633299

PRAISE FOR NAOMI NASH!

SENSES WORKING OVERTIME

"A good addition to most teen library collections."
—*KLIATT*

"With *Senses Working Overtime*, Naomi Nash reveals her talent for not only being able to weave an interesting, humorous teen novel, but a more serious teen novel…with drama galore…. Another winner for Naomi Nash!"
—Erika Sorocco, Teen Correspondent

BEANER O'BRIAN'S ABSOLUTELY GINORMOUS GUIDEBOOK TO GUYS

"This book is side-splitting funny! The story is attention-grabbing, and the book is sure to be a happy addition to your bookshelf. *Guidebook to Guys* is yet another out-of-the-park score for Naomi Nash."
—*Romance Reviews Today*

"A fun story."
—*RT BOOKclub*

"Naomi Nash has introduced us to many wonderful characters, but none have been as engaging, and enjoyable to read about as Beaner O'Brian."
—Erika Sorocco, Teen Correspondent

"A great read."
—*The Best Reviews*

MORE PRAISE FOR NAOMI NASH!

CHLOE, QUEEN OF DENIAL

"Smooch is setting the mark in quality young adult fiction, with this being no exception."
—*Huntress Reviews*

"Beautifully written, life-like, and features characters that really pull you into the story."
—*Romance Reviews Today*

YOU ARE SO CURSED!

"This book perfectly describes an alienated teenager in the hostile environment of high school. This tale is perfect for library shelves."
—*KLIATT*

"How can you go wrong with a book about a faux witch, a hot guy, a poop-crazy goat and those girls you just love to hate? ...This book finds a hilarious medium. Definitely recommended for the confused person in all of us."
—*RT BOOKclub*

"A marvelous book and a great addition to the Smooch line."
—*Romance Reviews Today*

PARTY GIRL

"There's this party, Saturday," I said to Gio, trying to sound offhanded about it.

"Yeah, Brandon Jerome's." Gio's body beneath his plaid shirt, where it rested against my back, was all the warmth I'd ever need. "He told me. Said we should come. What—wait a minute." He pulled away and looked at me in astonishment. "You didn't want to *go,* did you?"

"No!" I exclaimed, scornful. After a second, I reconsidered. "Did you?"

"Did you?" he asked, seeming doubtful. "I mean, we could, but I didn't think you'd want to." Oh, creeping crud. Tabitha had been right. Or was there another reason he hadn't wanted to invite me along? That crowd was prettier and better dressed and were able to bring their own lunches in neat little plastic receptacles. I didn't fit in with them. I never had. I never would. More than ever before, right then I felt like Gio might be editing me out of parts of his life. That realization very nearly made me stop walking.

"I think we should go." The words tasted like bitter medicine, but sometimes medicine was what you needed to make things better, right?

Other SMOOCH books by Naomi Nash:

SENSES WORKING OVERTIME
BEANER O'BRIAN'S ABSOLUTELY
**   GINORMOUS GUIDEBOOK TO GUYS**
CHLOE, QUEEN OF DENIAL
YOU ARE *SO* CURSED!

I AM *SO* JINXED!

NAOMI NASH

SMOOCH NEW YORK CITY

*In memory of Cameron Robb,
one of Vick Marotti's first fans and admirers.*

SMOOCH ®

February 2006

Published by

Dorchester Publishing Co., Inc.
200 Madison Avenue
New York, NY 10016

If you purchased this book without a cover you should be aware that this book is stolen property. It was reported as "unsold and destroyed" to the publisher and neither the author nor the publisher has received any payment for this "stripped book."

Copyright © 2006 by Vance Briceland

All rights reserved. No part of this book may be reproduced or transmitted in any form or by any electronic or mechanical means, including photocopying, recording or by any information storage and retrieval system, without the written permission of the publisher, except where permitted by law.

ISBN 0-8439-5405-1

The name "SMOOCH" and its logo are trademarks of Dorchester Publishing Co., Inc.

Printed in the United States of America.

Visit us on the web at www.smoochya.com.

I AM *SO* JINXED!

CHAPTER ONE

Right above her lip, Vice Principal Oostergard sported a quivering red mole that reminded me of a ladybug. Let me rephrase. Say some Hollywood big shots came up with a script for a horror movie about scientists who crossed killer bees with ordinary ladybugs— *Ladybugzzzz!*, or something like that—and they needed a model for the souped-up, fanged version. Specifically, a bulgy beetle with an enormous black hair sprouting from the middle of its back. I knew a vice principal with the real goods.

"Vickie?" If the sound of my name being mangled hadn't woken me right up, the death rattle of the 11:10 bell surely would have. The chairs in Oostergard's office weren't doing my butt any good, so I was glad to shift around and grab my backpack, ready to bolt. "You seem distracted."

Oh, she had no idea. "It's Vick," I reminded her for the umpteenth time. "Rhymes with *quick, slick,* and *chick*." Let adults have an inch, and they'd take a hemisphere. "It's my lunch period now, so . . ."

I don't know how vice principals are made. Does anyone really wake up one morning and decide, *Hey! I'm going to be a vice principal when I grow up! Woohoo!* Somehow I didn't think so. Wherever they came from, whether a vice principal boot camp or some kind of creepy bioengineering lab, all the vice principals I've known seemed to develop convenient Sudden Deafness Syndrome when I said something they didn't want to hear. Particularly when it came to my lunch. "Don't you like Vickie, dear?" No, I didn't. My name was Vick. I didn't like Vickie, I didn't like Victoria. I didn't like Vice Principal Oostergard's bleached perm or her plastic orange eyeglasses, her hairy ladybug mole, or the way she kept looking at my file with bugged-out eyes like it was some kind of hot 'n sexy novel and she needed a few minutes of alone time with it.

My backpack rested in my lap. My feet were in sprint position. My brain had already walked out of our new vice principal's office and through the main door to take a breather on the front steps of Millard Fillmore High School. All I needed was an official benediction, and my body could join it. Instead, my jailer leaned back in her chair and regarded me as if I were a sorry-looking papier-mâché volcano filled with baking powder and she were the science fair judge. "Vickie," she said, rubbing her fingertip on the mole. That so squicked me out. "One of the reasons Mr. Dermot didn't return this year is because the administration felt he wasn't adequately addressing the school's at-risk students. Your counselor, Mr. O'Doul, and I agree that one of my functions in this position . . ."

Blah, blah, blah. I'd thought being a junior would be a breeze with Vice Principal Dermot finally out of my hair. During my sophomore year, Dermot the Doormat had been the bane of my existence, constantly assuming I was behind everything bad that happened at school. Okay, maybe there'd been a few things where I might have had a hand. Like when I'd broken the nose off the bust of President Fillmore. Or the afternoon I'd kind of invaded the boys' showers while the guys from the softball team were lathering up. And the night when Rambo the Killer Mountain Goat, our school mascot, had gone on a rampage in the Doormat's office and topped it off with a stinking giftie that only a goat with an intestinal problem could deliver. Yeah, I might have been somewhere nearby. But none of those things had been *intentional*. Sometimes stuff just kind of happened. Actually, that goat poo incident had happened in the very office where I was now sitting.

Ew.

Six weeks ago, when I'd walked through the front doors of Fillmore and had taken my first lungful of Dermot-free air, I'd felt like pounding my chest, Tarzan-style, and yelling at the glorious freedom of it all. If I'd known I would be spending Monday mornings in special sessions with the Oostermonster, I might not have been so hasty to see Dermot's backside. At least his little confrontations had been short and sweet, and hadn't made me long for something to take away the tedium. Anything would have done. Chinese water torture or bamboo spikes beneath my nails would be more pleasant. Even Algebra II.

". . . remember what Mr. O'Doul has said about anger management techniques. Right?"

Uh-oh. A direct question. I wasn't prepared for one of those. "Um, deep breaths, in with anger, out with love, can I go to lunch now?" I improvised. "I only get forty minutes."

Simple yes-or-no question, right? Wrong. The Oostermonster let her fingers intertwine in one of those here-is-the-church, here-is-the-steeple, open-your-mouth-and-bore-all-the-people gestures. "How are things at home, Vickie?"

Oh, man. We were so not going there. I'm not a bad kid. I'm honestly not. I hadn't gotten into a lick of trouble since the beginning of the school year. If old Dermot hadn't fled the school and left on his desk a thick folder with my name on it, the new vice principal could have focused her attention on the smokers and bullies and stoners and cutters and hall-runners and cheaters and all the other kids who actually deserved to be sitting in that chair instead of on me, and I'd be a much happier Vick. My home life wasn't any of this woman's business. I let her know it with upraised eyebrows.

"Is there any progress with your father, dear?"

Progress? As if my dad were an invalid or something! "He's fine. I'm fine. Everything's fine." I looked at the clock on her desk. "It's going to take me about six minutes to get to the cafeteria, Ms. Oostergard, and already I'm five minutes late, and if I don't leave now, I'll have less than a half hour to eat, and studies say midday nutrition is essential for student performance . . ."

I stopped talking when, without warning, she un-
clenched her fingers and made a note on her pad. I
would've given anything to see what she'd written.
Defensive, probably. Maybe, *Avoids the issue at hand*.
Or quite possibly, *What a hog*. Despite a stab of interest, I gritted my teeth and waited for the lecture that
was surely going to follow. I got nothing, though,
save for the sound of her pencil scraping against paper. "I'd like it," she said at last, still writing, "if you
would tell your father that I will be calling him soon.
Just to check in." Oh, creeping crud. What'd she
want to go and do *that* for? Old, witchy Vick
would've squawked her head off about that injustice,
but autumn-fresh, magic-free Vick only smiled and
nodded. Finally, after a lot more scratching, she
looked up through her oversized clown glasses. "You
can go," she said at last, surprised to see me still
there. Somehow she managed to make it sound like
I'd been the one lounging around, taking up *her* time.

I didn't need a second invitation. I scrambled the
heck out of that office, with its motivational posters
and lavender-smelling potpourri, with a cheery, "Thank
you, Ms. Oostergard!" that made Mrs. Detweiler and
the other school secretaries look up from their desks
and smile my way. You see, there *are* some people in
the world who don't hold a grudge because you accidentally let the school mascot masticate their desk sup-
plies.

I said *masticate*. It's a verb. Look it up.

Anyway, if there was one thing New Vick still had in
common with Old Vick, it was attitude—and plenty of
it. Just because I wasn't using my mad sleight-of-hand

skills to pretend to be a witch didn't mean I'd lost my edge. I was still tough. When Dad and I had moved to this most pathetic of tiny cities out in the middle of the American Midworst last year, I'd dyed my hair as dark as I could, painted all my nails black, and smudged penciled kohl around my eyes. When I had turned and looked in the mirror, it felt like I'd finally found my real calling. Vickie the Timid, pushed around at school after school, had become Vick the Dangerous, the kind of girl the other kids avoided. The kind of girl they scarcely dared to look in the eye.

The kind of girl who still stalked her way down the hallway knowing she intimidated everyone. Yeah. The new, trouble-free Vick was a chick to keep away from, with her black jeans and black boots with red leather flames at the toes, and with the strings of her dark hoodie swinging as she approached a half dozen upperclassmen jocks clustered around a locker. They were the worst of the bunch, those muscle-boys with varsity jackets for brains, always picking on the helpless. Well, they surely weren't going to mess with . . .

"Yo, Marotti!" yelled one of the guys, turning around. Usually I didn't bother remembering names of the *hoi polloi*, but I recognized this one: Tyler Woodwell, football jock. Dangerously good-looking on the outside, but rotten to the core. His hand shot out so abruptly that my reflexes warned me of the imminent punch-down to come. Every finely honed instinct I possessed alerted me for a fight. I jumped around and landed on both feet in a defensive position, ready to dish back whatever mess he planned to serve.

That's when I realized his hand was raised in a high five position. He looked at me strangely. "Something wrong?"

"No." I scowled and tried to pretend I hadn't raised both my fists in the air, ready to whoop his sorry butt. Okay, so maybe he hadn't been about to slam me physically, but mental warfare was fair game to these jerks. I would've bet the $1.35 in my pocket that the next thing to come from his mouth would be a poison arrow aimed right at my heart. "Something wrong with *you*? Huh?"

"Nope," he said, seeming taken aback. That was what I wanted to hear—the sweet words of a tough guy backing down. He scratched his head through the gray wool cap he always wore. Weird. I hadn't noticed until now that Tyler was the only guy in his crew without the usual letter jacket. Most of those big-time athletes wore those things even to bed, didn't they? "You weren't in social studies last period. I was going to lend you my notes. There's a test on Friday."

Oh. I waited for a second, half-hoping for some kind of punch line to follow, or that he'd yank the outstretched offering away right as I reached for it. Yet the offer was real. "Thanks," I mumbled, stowing the notebook in the outer pocket of my backpack, feeling forty different kinds of foolish. That's not what rotten-to-the-core people did, usually. "That's kind of . . . nice of you."

He laughed. One of the other jockheads, Arnie Peterson, reached out and shoved me on the shoulder. Playfully. "For a minute there you looked like you were gonna beat him up!"

I had to stand there and grin and take it like a schmoe. "Yeah, well."

"Nah, man, Marotti wouldn't do that. She's cool. Right?" The way Tyler grinned at me you would've thought we were the best of buds. That went for his boneheaded friends, too. They all bared their teeth like I was an oversized banana and they were the zoo's chimp exhibit. Once again Tyler's hand was raised, waiting. Crud. I was going to have to do it. Slowly, reluctantly, I lifted my own, only to have him grab it and go through a whole secret soul shake routine. The locked thumbs, the curved fingers, the elbow bump, everything. When I finally escaped and started making my way down the hall again, I smelled all testosterone-y. I was one of the guys. The only thing standing between me and a varsity jacket of my own was a pair of Air Maxes and a tube of tough-actin' Tinactin. "Hey, Marotti," Tyler called out, as I separated from the group with a grunt. "Let's hang out sometime, bro."

"Sure, bro," I said through my teeth, though in my head I was thinking, *unlikely, sis.*

Okay, so maybe those guys weren't scared of me anymore. But you know, they were merely a portion of the whole school. One of the crown cliques, sure, but not the only ones who mattered. By the time I rounded the corner near the art rooms and the wood shop, heading down the hallway past a rehearsal room where I could hear the jazz band tooting away, my swagger was back. I'd found my center of gravity—a burning ball of fire in my gut. I was tough. I looked out for myself. Nobody messed with me.

When I walked by, people recognized that my exterior was impenetrable armor. I was an enigma. Inscrutable. A sphinx of whom no one asked any questi—

Aauugh! Had I accidentally disturbed some kind of feminine beehive? Without warning I was swarmed by girls, all of them bright as Japanese candy wrappers and smelling of perfume and fruity lip gloss. "Oh my God! Would you look at *her?*" DeMadison Cook, de facto leader of the fashionable girls' set ever since her best friend transferred to a private school after last year, thrust forward her head until it was only inches from my face. What was I, her freakin' science project? "Vick, *where* did you get that eye shadow?"

Oh, fan-diddly-tastic. I was going to have to endure taunts about my face from the wenches who had made my life a living hell last year. I opened my mouth, ready to let loose my switchblade tongue on their pampered little hineys. No, not literally. Then Tabitha Hunter, she of the beautiful chestnut hair so perpetually flat and perfect that I suspected she'd obtained it only after performing a little daily morning routine involving conditioner, smoothing gel, and the ritual sacrifice of an unblemished lamb, leaned in and studied me, too. "Does it have glitter?"

"It *does!*" DeMadison said, reaching up a finger toward my eye. I could flinch away, but I couldn't run. I was surrounded by fembots. "It's *adorable!* Where did you *get* it?"

Nuh-uh. No way. There was no chance that I was going to be all girly-girl with this bunch. Not my scene, not my style. "I haven't seen anything like it at the mall,"

Tabitha announced. "Now, Vick, your look's what they call Goth, right? I am *so* thinking of going Goth next month," she told her Bonne Bell buddies.

"Don't be *silly*." Before I could reply, DeMadison had flung her arm around my shoulder. "When my parents and I were in Lincoln over the summer, I saw lots of girls like Vick at the coffee shops. Goth is *over*. Vick is *post-Goth,* which is way cooler. Right, Vick?"

While she launched into a mini-lecture about the differences between—well, whatever, I really didn't care—my head started to swim. Partly it was because the overabundance of J.Lo Glow and A&F Now with which they'd spritzed themselves deprived my lungs of oxygen. Mostly it was because I couldn't believe that *the* most popular set of girls at Millard Fillmore High was discussing my appearance without using the words *freak*, *nasty*, or *skank*. All semester I'd noticed they weren't as noxious as last year, but from where came this unearned chumminess? Maybe I'd stumbled into Bizarro School, where everything was backwards from reality. Maybe I was Bizarro Vick. If I looked at myself in the mirror right now, I might have perfectly styled hair, shiny lips, and creamy cover-girl skin.

But no. When some girl whose name I hadn't bothered to learn reached out to twiddle the rose quartz pendant I wore around my neck ("Where did you *get* that?"), I knew that things might be bizarro, but my booted feet were firmly stuck in reality. I wasn't some kind of post-Goth fashion spread in *J-14* or *Teen People* to be picked over and copied. I didn't even know what the heck post-Goth was. I mean, Goth was over when I lived on the West Coast years ago, and if the stuff I was wearing was appearing in the trendy coffee shops of Lincoln, Nebraska, maybe it was time for me to hang it up and go nude.

Only that would involve other people actually having to see my private bits. I pulled my pendant from the wench's painted talons. "That was a gift," I told her. That quartz was the one tangible thing that meant something to me, and I didn't want it tugged on. Then, to DeMadison, I said, "I've got to get to the cafeteria. I've only got twenty minutes before . . ."

"Oh. My. God," DeMadison announced, putting her hands on my forearm. "I hope you brought your lunch. You brought your lunch, right? Because the smells from the lunch line today—you will ralph." With a pair of fingers, she mimed gagging herself.

"Yeah, I'll take that into consideration." Right about the time I'd consider adopting a six-foot python, which was no time soon. Were they walking with me? To my utter dismay, I saw that they were. I'd attracted a little entourage that followed me past the last of the band practice rooms in the direction of the cafeteria. Sadly, DeMadison seemed to be right about the cafeteria stench. Roadkill would have smelled better, sprinkled with garlic and motor oil and left to broil in the summer sun until a bubbly medium rare.

Six months before, these girls would sooner have spat on than talked to me. Those football jocks? Given half a chance, they would've wiped their muddy cleats on my backside and used my homework for toilet paper. My friends and I had spent all of last year as outcasts, the lowest of the low; not a day had gone by when I hadn't had to extricate one of us from the strangleholds of these chuckleheads. And if they weren't beating us up in the bathrooms, or tripping us in the hallways, they were whispering behind our backs in class or mocking us in the locker rooms.

Suddenly this year, I was everybody's friend? Unlikely! None of it made sense. Not that I had the remotest chance of reflecting on anything with DeMadison's unending chatter in my ear. ". . . you had Iverson last year, didn't you, Vick?" she was saying, dabbing at my elbow so much that I had to check to see if there was a bug there she was trying to shoo away, or something. "He is *so* hard. I was saying to Brandon Jerome . . . you know Brandon, don't you? Ohmigod, you've *got* to come to his party a week from Saturday."

Me, attend a party? A senior boy's kegger? Unlikely: The Sequel. "I'm busy."

Professor Plum showing up in the conservatory with the lead pipe right then couldn't have been a bigger clue, right? Somehow it went right over all their heads. Tabitha and Sophia Glews and Zoe Moore and all the rest began begging me to reconsider. Worst of all was DeMadison. "Oh, *come!*" she pleaded. "His folks are out of town! I'll do your hair!"

What a freak-tabulous prospect. Anyone who knew me knew I had a thing about alcohol abuse. Throw in the hullabaloo of sub-primates, *and* a girly-girl doing my hair, and what could I say? What was the tactful way to tell her a triple root canal sounded more attractive? "It'll be fun," Tabitha told me from my other side. We were only a little ways from the cafeteria by this point. Knowing that in a couple of minutes I'd have a legitimate reason to break away from them was the only thing keeping me sane. "Everyone who's anyone will be there."

I was never going to escape these chicks. Future archaeologists were going to discover my fossilized skeleton in a fetal position surrounded by their own delicately arranged desiccated bodies, as if I'd stumbled into an unusually feminine chain gang partial to leg shaving and cotton candy–flavored lip gloss. "Aw, what a pity I'm nobody, huh?" I'm not sure how I'd expected them to react to that statement, but the chorus of coos and laughter wasn't it. Those dames thought I was being funny! "Well," I finally said, turning around. This weird little circus parade couldn't go on any longer. "Gotta chow down. Smell ya later." Oh crap. Irene was pouting. I'd actually made someone pout?

"Ladies." A gruff voice made me whip around again, only to find a burly guy standing behind me. Well, a burly someone who might easily pass as a guy, if you didn't know what Ray was all about. He reached up and stroked the pencil-thin circle of facial hair growing around his mouth. "*Lovely* ladies," he added, saying the words as if they were so tasty that he had to savor them first. I looked at him, suspicious. Was he trying to act smooth? He was! He so was! For one thing, he was dressed like a big player—long chocolate brown suede jacket, and pants and cap that matched exactly, the cap pointed off the side of his head. Big brown rimless square sunglasses. That ghost of a goatee. Was it drawn on? If so, it was really convincing.

From behind me, I heard giggles. Those girls were laughing at Ray! Nothing could have more gotten my goat, and I didn't mean Rambo the Killer Mountain Goat, either. "Let's go," I told him, grabbing his arm.

"What's the hurry?" He slid off his shades, wiped them on the front of his shiny shirt, and leered at De-Madison. She responded with a little dip of her knees and a clenched hand in front of her mouth. That witch was *totally* trying not to laugh at him, and he wasn't letting me hustle him away. Hadn't I protected him all last year from these losers? "Maybe you could introduce me to your friends— Hey!" The last protest was for the way I yanked him away and dragged him behind me toward the cafeteria doors. "What'd you do that for?"

Kids were always milling around the cafeteria entrance, overflowing from it into the hallway as they talked and laughed and carried on. At least a good two dozen people had seen the way I'd manhandled one of my best friends, and watched us now from the corners of their eyes. I didn't care. "Why are you acting so weird?" I wanted to know. Even over the hubbub of the lunchtime crowd, I knew Ray could hear me. As well as just about everybody else. "They were laughing at you!"

Ray's eyes slitted. His arms crossed. Gone was Pimp-Daddy Ray of a few minutes before. "No, they weren't. That's called 'flirting,' FYI. What's the problem with getting in on your action?" he asked.

They'd been flirty? That possibility had never occurred to me. I blinked. "I don't know what you're talking about." When someone gives me the *duh!* face, it never fails to exasperate. "I don't! What action?"

"Your stock's been up. Since, you know. That face-off with Melinda Scott last year?" I was used to Ray's brief little pronouncements. He was a poet, after all, and probably knew better than anyone how to express himself in the least amount of syllables. Problem was, I wasn't getting it. When I shrugged, he practically blew me over with the strength of his sigh. "Don't make me say the words."

"Say them!" I wondered if the Oostermonster would put strangulation on my permanent record. Probably. Ray gave me the slumped shoulder, the exaggerated sigh, the rolled eyes, the whole three-dollar routine. I gritted my teeth. "If you don't come out and say it, I swear to God, Ray . . ."

"Okay! But you already know. Things are different this semester, now you're all *popular*."

Ray said the words like they were the final conclusion to a geometry proof, but they struck me with the force of a hard slap. "Take it back," I warned, my voice small.

"Can't. You're popular. There's nothing wrong . . ." No more. I shook my head and walked away in mid-sentence. "V!" I heard him call at my back.

Nuh-uh. Those were the absolute last words I ever wanted to hear.

CHAPTER TWO

The noise in our lunchroom? It could deafen a girl, thanks to the low ceilings and the glass skylights that bounced every little sound right back down to the floor. The smell? The gacky odor of formaldehyde and dead fetal pig had been more appealing in biology last year. Without any teachers around and without tests and pop quizzes and labs and the insane pressure of field hockey to worry about, you'd think lunch might be the least insane part of the school day. But no. For a lot of people, lunch is when it's time to do the last-minute homework neglected the night before. It's also the period where you have to confront people you've been avoiding, or where you try desperately to squeeze in a little face time with friends you've been wanting to see all day. Between the shrieks and the yells and the haunted eyes of the homework-neglecters, the cafeteria seemed like one big teen abattoir.

Abattoir. It's the fancy word for a slaughterhouse. You know, where the animals go in as moo-cows and pop out as cheesesteaks and Slim Jims? Before my dad lost his job a couple of months before, I used to stay up late with the TV on for company and wait for him to come home. Once I saw a documentary on slaughterhouses that was so disgusting I turned vegetarian. For a week, anyway, until I went to the mall and heard a corndog whimpering my name. What I learned, though, is that school cafeterias and abattoirs are pretty similar. Both places fatten up inmates with institutional swill, line us up, and expect us to stumble blindly toward whatever axe is about to fall next—and those axes always fell eventually. I fingered the quartz around my neck. Knowing it hung there always gave me reassurance.

Ugh. The cafeteria lady dumped a plate of fish sticks onto my tray. They *were* trying to kill me.

My crew sat at the cafeteria's very back corner, under the window that dripped in wet weather. Our table seemed to be getting fuller lately, but my friends always saved a space for me right at its head. "How about The Seven?" Brie Layton acknowledged me with a nod. She and my best friend Addy were engaged in some kind of deep, philosophical discussion. They'd been doing that a lot lately. Addy shook her head. "Oh, come on." Like me, Brie had started out in Los Angeles. Unlike me, she still dressed the part; she always looked as if she'd recently run a credit card marathon at the Beverly Center. "I know you saw that movie about that girl who hits her head when she's thirteen and wakes up and she's practically menopausal and a magazine editor, and . . ."

Maybe this conversation wasn't so deep or philosophical, after all. "We saw it together," Addy reminded her. She smiled to show she wasn't totally ignoring me. I didn't mind. They'd all finished their meals, and I hadn't begun. I tore open a few little packets of ketchup and mustard and began to swirl them together in a puddle. Addy obviously was trying to do some kind of review for later in the day; she had a list of chemical equations she was busily trying to balance. "Remember? Vick and Gio and us two went."

"But you and I were the only ones *watching*." Trust me, I knew exactly what Brie meant by that snarky little comment, but I wasn't biting anything save my fish sticks. What was that weird, gooey yellow stuff sitting to their side? Macaroni and cheese, maybe? "Anyway, the snotty girls in the movie called themselves The Six. So like, we could be The Seven. You, me, Gio, Vick, Dorie, Desiree, Ray." It said something about Brie that although she'd ticked off seven people on her fingers, she still managed to land on her pinkie.

"But there are lots more of us, now," Addy pointed out, not looking up from her homework. "There's Little Tony, Marvella, and lots of others." A couple of other kids farther down the table looked around at the sound of their names, then went back to their talking. "I thought you hated the hot lunches here," she added to me.

I shrugged, avoiding the question by shoving in a mouthful of lukewarm fish. "They're all right."

"I meant the *original* seven."

That was enough to get Addy to look up. She ran a

hand through her long, straight red hair. "I don't want to be named after snotty girls. And if you want to be technical, Brie, you're not really part of the original group." *Attagirl, Addy*, I thought to myself, gobbling away. My theory was that the quicker I ate the swill on my plate, the less I'd actually have to taste it. *Sock it to her.* "That would have been me, Vick, Dorie, Des, and Ray. You and Gio didn't come along until last spring. Hey. You've been eating school lunches every day."

Oh, creeping crud. With that last sentence, she was back to me again. I really didn't need the attention, particularly on this issue. She was absolutely right. I'd had a cafeteria lunch every day for weeks now, and I'd hoped no one would ever notice. So much for that. Maybe I could throw her off the scent. "Nuh-uh." When I checked to see if she was buying my bold-faced lie (she wasn't), I countered with another. "I've been getting up late in the mornings."

"Too late to shove your dad's takeout leftovers into a paper bag?" It wasn't polite to respond with your mouth full, right? I shoved in some more mac and cheese. The days of late-night leftovers had ended along with my dad's full-time employment, but what Addy didn't know about my home life wouldn't hurt her.

"I think it's a good name." Brie was still off in her own little la-la land. I'd lived in cities all over the country, starting with the biggest and getting progressively smaller as my dad chased job after job, until we'd ended up here. No matter where you were, though, you could always tell the California girls. Time moved differently for them. Even in the middle of the American heartland, where the buffalo actually did roam and where instead of vast flat plains of suburbs, we had amber waves of grain and purple mountains majesty right outside the city limits, Brie always managed to give the impression she was only stopping off for a quick chai before an afternoon shopping on Rodeo Drive. Then again, maybe she simply didn't want to be reminded of the fact that last year, when she'd been a new student, she'd been one of the enemy. "Okay, how about the Phonics?"

"Inane," Addy said, returning to her equations.

I'd consumed the bulk of the cremains passing as my lunch, so I stopped chewing to ask the obvious question. "Exactly what are you guys talking about?"

When Addy shook her head and went back to balancing, I suspected they had to be discussing something silly. And boy, was I righter than right. Brie put aside a wrap bursting with lettuce and falafel and hummus so she could make her point. "I was saying—um." I could tell by the way Brie couldn't look at me that whatever it was, it was going to be stupid. "That our clique should have a name."

"No." It's not that Brie and I were enemies exactly. Maybe once, a long time ago, when she'd been new and trying to feel her way around, but not now. We hung out, we went to movies, we watched TV and did homework together. We were friendly. Just not always friends. Or was it the other way around?

"Oh, come on." The words came bursting out. She must have been anticipating that I'd shut her down.

"Last year you guys had a name for DeMadison and that crew."

"We called you guys The Hair Club For Harpies because you deserved it." I honestly hadn't intended to include Brie in that pronouncement, but somehow it came popping out. She looked a little taken aback. Aw, heck. I honestly hadn't intended to stomp on anyone's feelings. "They, I mean. Not you. Them. Anyway, it was our nickname. They didn't call themselves that."

I could have taken my apology further, but Brie didn't seem seriously annoyed. Besides, it's kind of difficult to talk when you suddenly have four feet seven inches of freshman lounge lizard sidling next to you. "Call themselves what, baby?" Little Tony asked, fanning himself with a comic book in what he probably thought was a sexy way.

Addy glanced at the comic book's cover, which featured some guy's face melting under a superhero's eye-beam, in full color. "I thought your mom didn't let you buy those."

"Fuhgeddaboutit!" he said, snapping his fingers.

I turned to face my favorite shrimp. "Tony?"

"Yeah, dollface?" You know how some boys consider it their life's sole purpose to make a girl wish she hadn't combed her hair or put on her face that morning? That was Little Tony in a nutshell. He didn't make me feel dirty, the way some of the senior boys sometimes used to when they were on one of their über-macho, chest-beating, testosterone binges. He did, however, act like a not-so-secret agent given the assignment to track down and assassinate my last remaining nerve. He leaned over and leered, exposing a mouth full of hardware. "What can Little Tony do ya for?"

Whenever Desiree's freshman brother invaded my personal space, Addy got a funny little smirk on her face. Although she pretended to be working her way through those last-minute equations, her lips twitched. As for me, I couldn't decide whether I was more annoyed by Tony's continued public insistence that we were an item, or by the fact that his lower braces seemed to have trapped about half of his peanut-butter-and-banana sandwich. "What can Little Tony do me for?" I repeated. If I beaned him on the head with one of the fish sticks, would that merit another trip to the Oostermonster's office? On second thought, those sticks were like cement, and the kid had ample brain damage already. "Tony, you're like one of ten African-American kids in this white-bread school. You couldn't run with that? You have to pretend you're one of the Sopranos?"

"You inspire me, my little rigatoni."

I could have taken a handful of Velveeta, wadded it up, slathered it in Gorgonzola, dipped it in melted Swiss, and sprinkled it with parmesan, and I still wouldn't have as big a cheeseball as Tony. "Des," I called down to the far end of the table, where Desiree and Dorie were holding court with some of their friends. "I think it's time your baby brother's diapers got changed."

What'd I get for that smart remark? A little laugh and a wave. Thanks bunches, Desiree. A year ago, when these guys were dependent on me for every-thing, it would have been different. Hoo boy, would it ever! Des had always been sweet and loveable, the kind of girl that no one could really dislike if they got to know her, but she had been so high-strung and nervous that she'd chewed at her lips until they were scabby and bitten the ends of her fingers until they were bloody and raw, like tuna tartare.

That's uncooked fish on a plate that they serve at fancy restaurants. Don't ask me how I know. It's a grim story. Swanky dinner. First real outing with my boyfriend and his parents. Four brave bites, then a half hour of yakking and regrets in the restroom. Trust me, no matter what your boyfriend's mom says, it's nothing like Chicken of the Sea.

Little Tony still leered at me. "You gonna do the changing, sweetcheeks?" My hand was so quick that he didn't see it coming. One swift arm around his shoulders and suddenly his face was three inches from mine. Anyone else in that crowded cafeteria would have thought the two of us were huddled in some kind of buddy-buddy confabulation that no lunchroom monitor or wandering vice principal might have misconstrued as hostile. But it was a strangle-hold, all right. After fifteen seconds of swearing and swatting at me with his comic book, he squawked out, "Come on, Marotti! I know you're a marshmal-low beneath that—hey!" The kid was so tiny that I had a way unfair physical advantage over him. Heck, a pair of wet long johns flapping on a clothesline could have taken him out. "You know they say that

acts of aggression are really a sign of true lov—gack!"
Again I tightened the neckhold. "All right, all right,
name your terms, dollface!"

Teeth bared into a replica of a perfect smile, I
yanked him closer. "One. Stop calling me *dollface*."

"Whatever you want, sweet—ow! Okay! Okay!"

"Two," I said, maintaining my grip. "Give up on the
idea that you and I will ever be an item."

"I can't do that." When I gave him the ol' stink-eye,
he protested. "I can't! You're the woman for me!"

"I'm two whole years ahead of you," I pointed out.
"Not to mention a world of experience."

"I might be tiny, but I'm gonna shake up that
world, baby," he said, trying to break free. His strug-
gle was as weak as his lines.

"A world of hurt is what you're going to be in if
you keep it up," I warned.

Brie spoke up. "I think it's cute." At my sharp look
of disbelief, she straightened up. "Well, I do! He's like
one of those Munchkins in *The Wizard of Oz*, all
dressed up in big people clothes and trying to be . . .
Only he's not, obviously. You know what I mean!"

It's one thing for Little Tony to make fun of his own
size. There was no getting around the fact that for his
age, he was probably the tiniest person in the school,
male or female. But you know, a message went out
long ago saying that there are certain groups that stupid people make fun of, whether it's because of looks
or skin color or simply because they're different, and
while it's okay for the people inside those groups to
joke about their differences, it's not right for anyone
else to call attention to it. Brie apparently never got

that memorandum. Tony seemed to shrink even more, so much that my neck lock loosened and he slipped under my arm. "Brie!" I growled. Tony could be a pain in the butt, especially when he was pretending to have a fake crush on me, but someone else being a pain right back didn't cancel it out. It all added up to one massive butt-ache.

"It *is* cute!" she protested.

Tony still smarted from her remark. I ran through my list of options. Hug him? Too patronizing. Pat him on the arm? Not much in the way of consolation. Rub him on the back? He'd probably like that too much. I settled for a smile. He was a kid, after all. "I still don't see what Gio's got that I don't got," he muttered.

"Hmmm, let's see. He's got three years on you, he's college bound, and he holds the keys to a shiny blue Mustang," I said, ticking finger after finger. "How's that for starters?"

"I knew it was the Mustang that kept you with me," I heard over my shoulder. "Good thing I got that instead of the econo-box my folks picked out, huh?"

My heart leapt up at the sound of Gio Carson's familiar voice, and my body followed. From zero to arms around his neck in 1.5 seconds flat—a new world record! Then I remembered myself. Despite the fact that Brie and Addy and Little Tony and all the other kids at the table, not to mention everyone at the far end of the noisy lunchroom, had seen me leap up and throw myself onto possibly the school's most delicious guy, I stepped off my tiptoes and pretended I'd only stood up to scratch the back of my head. "Hey," I said. La, la, la. I was cool. I wasn't one of those girls who had to be throwing herself on her guy all the time. I fiddled with the rose quartz around my neck that he'd given me for my birthday.

"Hey, you." Gio liked when I wore his gift, so I always kept it around my neck, to remind myself how lucky I was some other girl hadn't yet lured him away.

Oh, by all that was sweet and sacred, what his smiles did for me. "Hey." Yes, I was fully aware I'd hey-ed him a moment before. No, I didn't care.

Unlike Addy and Brie and, well, just about everyone else with whom I'd gone through sophomore year, I hadn't opted for A.P. Chem. Instead, because of "home life stresses," the Oostermonster had seen to it that I'd been placed in Physics for Boneheads with a bunch of kids who had more tattoos than brain cells to rub together. It was a joke of a class, but one of the things we'd been doing the past week was playing with prisms. You know, those triangular, transparent things? When you take one and hold it up to a window during the daytime, something happens. The ordinary, ho-hum light passes through and splits into brilliant colors, each one pure, each one shimmering. Of course all those hues are part of ordinary light all the time, but a prism reveals them in all their glory.

Gio made me feel exactly like that, inside. All my colors shone whenever he came around. "You look good."

Is it bad that I went all girly on the inside when he said that? When other kids, and most adults, toted up my makeup and my dark hair and my ragged clothing and calculated me to be a nobody—or worse, post-Goth—Gio always seemed to accept me as I was.

Everything he said came out sounding so simple and sincere. It was impossible not to trust those wide-open brown eyes. Or want to run your fingers through that short, spiky blond hair. Or grab him around the waist and pull him toward you and kind of—well. I cleared my throat. "Eh. Thanks though." I liked that he squeezed my hand to let me know he'd meant it. "Want to sit?" I asked, sliding back down.

He looked along the table length. "There's not really a lot of room at the old table lately, is there?"

"What do you mean?" Why was I playing dumb? I knew full well what he meant; I was shoving away at Tony with my foot underneath the table to make space. For some reason, I couldn't bring myself to admit the truth. And yet it came popping out. "It's not like we're suddenly popular over here or anything." The word *popular* came out sounding like I had raked my teeth over it.

Gio raised an eyebrow at that. "Tony, my man," he said, sitting down on the few vacated square inches. I retrieved my foot just in time. The two guys went through some kind of complicated handshake ritual that Brie and I watched in fascination. Even Addy looked over the top of her book. What was it with guys and their weird soul shakes? "Vick beating you up again?"

"Naw." Tony seemed a little shy at Gio's attention. "She's all right."

"You don't know how all right, little man. How'd that algebra thing go? Good?"

Little Tony let loose with a big, wide smile at that question. "Yeah! Thanks!"

Gio rewarded him with a bump of the elbow. "Excellent." Hero worship in action: Though he'd been grumpy a few seconds before at having to give up his place to Gio, Tony now practically panted like a puppy dog after his master. I think there's a technical, psychological term all the best psychiatrists use for that kind of behavior: *pathetic*.

"So are we on for later tonight?" I asked.

Gio's lips twisted into a pout. A handsome pout. I loved that pout. I wanted a photo of that pout for my back pocket, so I could look at it whenever I wanted. "I've got work at the senior . . ."

". . . the senior center, I know." Sure, community service looked good on his record. But darn those old folks! They'd hogged him since the semester's start! "Tomorrow night, too?"

"Every night this week. All Saturday, too." Ouch. He must've seen my expression, because he tried to console me. "Hey," he said, putting an arm around my shoulders and hugging me close. His chin rested on my shoulder as he stared at me. "If I put in enough hours now, I'll have a certificate for my folder before college apps are due. Once those are all in, I'll have plenty of time. And we'll be spending it together. You and me."

I liked his consolation, coming as it did in the form of a tight hug. "Okay," I said, for him alone. "I'm busy Saturday, anyway."

"Sunday night, maybe? We could hit the movies. We haven't been to the movies in a long time."

Mmmm. Gio liked the movies. He liked the action on the screen and the darkness, where we could hold hands and, you know, indulge in a little bit of light smooching if the story got boring. Unfortunately for the health of my wallet, movies had been kind of out of the question for a few weeks now. I tried to dodge the issue. "We could watch a DVD at your place. Curl up on the sofa, have some popcorn?"

"The usual? Sure." If he was disappointed, it didn't show. "What's with you and all these cafeteria lunches lately, anyway? I thought you hated them."

Crud. Of all the topics! Why was everyone noticing now something that had been going on since the beginning of the year? "They're not that bad," I lied, pretending that most of the glop the hair-netted cafeteria lady had scooped onto my plate wasn't still there . . . only twice as cold as before.

Gio studied me for a moment or two longer than was comfortable. "Are you okay?" he asked.

"Fine!" I said, keeping my voice light and bright. Gio shrugged. He believed me, didn't he? With everything he had going on, he didn't need to hear the whole sordid truth.

"Dude, when are we going to hang out again?" Despite my illusion of privacy, Little Tony had been hanging onto every word. I felt a little embarrassed. Pre-Gio, I'd always sneered when others indulged in PDA, and I didn't want suddenly to be the Queen of Public Smooching simply because I now had a boyfriend. It bugged me when people's personalities completely changed after they hooked up with someone. But I wasn't ungrateful for the change of topic. "You and me," he said to Gio. "*Mano a mano*."

"Real soon, bro," Gio promised the freshman. "I

know, I know, I owe you, okay?" Tony nodded. "All right, kids," he said, standing up. "I've got to load some photos onto the yearbook server."

"I don't get how you have time for everything you do." Addy, from the other side of the table, sounded a little envious. "Did someone give you a thirty-hour day or something?"

"It helps that his parents won't let him get a job," I said, slightly jealous myself.

"Hey, they want me focused on my academics." Gio winked at Addy. "Anyway, good time management helps. See you," he said to me, giving me a peck on the cheek and the slightest of waves before he disappeared in the crowd.

Tony acted as if the good-bye had been meant for him. "Later, bro!" he yelled at Gio's back.

I really couldn't blame Tony's hero worship at all. Gio was one of those people it was nearly impossible to find objectionable; it was almost as if he'd taken a bath in some secret government formula for sheer charisma. Everybody liked Gio. To the jocks he was a buddy who listened to their stories. To the A-list girls, he was someone to invite to parties. Parents doted on him and wished he were their own. A flash of those Colgate whites and he had the school staff eating out of his hand.

And my friends? They currently were drooling over him. At the table's far end I saw both Dorie and Desiree's head swivel as Gio left. Addy's gaze lingered, too. Brie sighed outright. "He's so yummy. Well, he *is!*" she added, when I looked at her with warning written in every wrinkle of my frown. "I'm not going to snatch him from you or anything. As if."

To my surprise, Addy sighed as well. "He *is* yummy." You know the way fish press their mouths against the aquarium glass and pucker their mouths? That's probably the way I looked at that moment. Practical Addy Kornwolf, she of the 4.0 grade average, the slate of AP classes, and a no-boys policy since a bad dating experience last year? Gaping at my guy? "Oh, Vick," she said. "Get over it. If you think other girls aren't going to look at Gio . . ."

"Or his hot little butt," Brie murmured, making me blink.

Addy narrowed her eyes. "Reel it in, lust-puppy," she told Brie. Then to me, she said, "We're only human. And he's adorable. Besides, I think you like that everyone's kind of hot for him."

"I do not!" I said, loudly as possible. In the noisy lunchroom, it didn't make much of an impact. Neither Addy nor Brie seemed to believe me. "Well, I don't!"

"She does," Brie said to Addy, who nodded. "You can tell."

"It's a compliment when other girls like your guy. Not when they try to hook up with him, mind you. Just when they admire." That was Addy through and through, trying to make bad news sound comforting.

"Oh yeah, totally," Brie agreed. "You should enjoy it for what it is." Enjoy it? Hah! To me, that threat was a combo crouching tiger and hidden dragon, ready to pounce. I didn't want other girls looking at Gio. I knew that was impossible for me to control, and I knew that if I thought about it too much, the ugly side of my jealousy might come roaring out. Gio was on the fast track to the college of his choice, followed by a lifetime of successes. Why should any of it include me? I asked myself that question daily. "Plus when you're associated with a guy like that, it makes you, you know. Popular."

Oooo, that word again. Three simple syllables shouldn't make a girl feel so angry, but I barely could control the emotions I felt at the sound. I wanted to throw something. Popularity meant changing to fit in. It meant selling out. There was no way I'd ever do that. My crew wouldn't, either.

Yet our lunch table had been empty last year, hadn't it? The only friends we'd had were each other. And I'd certainly never had the Hair Club girls asking me for fashion tips. Something *had* changed, but I didn't want to think too closely about what. If I searched too hard for the answer, I might have to admit Gio was the cause. I didn't want that to be the case. "What're you talking about?" Little Tony said. "You guys have always been popular."

Instead of answering Brie or throttling Tony, I glared at them both, gathered my tray and backpack, then stood up. "Don't bother giving this group a name," I told them. "The one I have in mind? The Oostermonster would have my head on a pole if I said it aloud. So yeah. I'll spare you this time."

Brie didn't talk again until I had my back turned and had started to stalk away. "I liked her better when she was pretending to be a witch," I heard her comment. "She was more fun then."

I Am *SO* Jinxed!

I couldn't give a *what* to the *ev* to the *er*. Fun or not, those days were long gone; there was only one place where I exercised my mad magic skills these days, and it wasn't in the school corridors.

CHAPTER THREE

"When I plunge my trusty magic wand—or a reasonable substitute—through the card. . . ." With a deft twist of the wrist, I skewered the Ace of Spades where it stood upright in the little plastic frame. "Hey presto!"

"Yeah, that's what happens when you push a pencil through something." I'd played a lot of tough audiences, but the little eleven-year-old on the other side of the counter was one tough cookie to impress. She stood with her arms crossed and an expression on her face like my grandma in Seattle used to wear if I belched during supper. "Want to know what happens if you jam it in your ear? You bleed. A lot." She rolled her eyes at another little girl beside her. Neither of them looked astonished.

I ignored the comment, instead lifting the little plastic stand and turning it so that she could see the pencil had indeed gone all the way through. The imp's name was Martina; she'd been a regular visitor to

Novel Tees since I'd started working there. Her buddy was new, though. "Now!" I said, putting it back down again, "Watch!" Like a surgeon—or at least someone who had gone for the funny bone in the game of Operation more times than she could count—I extracted the pencil.

"Wow! Look at that!" From behind the girls, Tabitha Hunter, the third spectator to my little show, clapped her hands together with excitement. My classmate really wasn't stupid, much as I wanted to think. She was trying to be helpful by whipping up a little enthusiasm with my peewee audience. "Fantastic!" Raving maniacs looked saner than she did. She was so excitable she looked like a kindergarten teacher who'd had one too many Dairy Queen MooLattes.

"That's not the end of the trick, monkey butt." Mouthy Martina's scorn could have withered granite.

Tabitha looked put out. "Monkey *hmmm* isn't a very nice word!" I guessed right then that Tabitha probably never had been sent to the principal's office for swearing.

The other evil munchkin giggled. "*Monkey butt.*"

A Mensa meeting, it was not. "Anyway," I said, trying to get focus back on my trick. "Notice how I can see all the way through?" I lowered my head down to the counter and peeked through the hole.

"Amazing!" raved Tabitha. What in the heck was she doing in the store, anyway? Mr. Schecter didn't usually like it when my friends hung around Novel Tees while I worked. Scratch that. Mr. Schecter really didn't care one way or the other, but *I* didn't like having people witness my humiliation at the hands of Western capitalism.

Mall sounds echoed through the store's entryway. From time to time, when the crowds were moving in the right direction, they'd bring with them food court smells that made my stomach growl. It had already been a long, long day. While I attempted to pretend that Tabitha existed in some alternate universe where people with perfect hair didn't dare to be seen hanging around people with snarly mops like mine, I wrapped my fingers around the plastic stand, contents and all, and pulled out the card. "Ta-daaaaa!" When I held out the ace, it was intact. No hole marred the giant spade in the card's center. "Amazing, huh?" I said, deliberately keeping my enthusiasm low so I didn't hop, skip, and cartwheel into Tabitha-the-cheerleader territory.

While my classmate applauded wildly, Martina scrunched up her face. "It's a trick."

"Well, duh," I said, good-naturedly. If Martina wanted to part with her hard-earned allowance every few weeks for a new gimmick to show her friends, I wasn't going to alienate her with real snark. "What do I look like, Samantha Stevens?"

"Cousin Serena," Tabitha said, unexpectedly. Then, apology written over her face, she added, "She was always my favorite. She was, you know. Kind of funky. Like you."

Tabitha really was Millard Fillmore High School's best living argument for hiring time-traveling renegades who could take themselves back to the night someone was conceived in order to put garlic in her parent's food and sprinkle itching powder in their bed so any chance of conception was out of the question. Me, Martina, and her monkey butt–loving little friend all gaped at her for a long time, until finally I spoke up. "Um, why don't you go look at the T-shirts or something while I take care of my customer?" Surely Tabitha couldn't miss the emphasis I'd placed on that particular word.

No, she hadn't. "Oh, okay!" she said, holding a finger to her lips and then going into a pantomime intended to let me know she was going to take a break and let me work. Or maybe that she needed to pee. Hard to tell. Charades obviously wasn't one of her stronger skills.

With that distraction finally gone, Martina and I got down to brass tacks, as they say. "How'd you do it?" she wanted to know.

I crossed my arms, tilted my head to the side, and gave her the ol' hairy eyeball. "Come on," I chided. "No way I'm telling." She seemed about ready to argue. "You know the rules. Buy the gimmick, or else figure it out for yourself."

We'd been through this routine many times during the four months I'd been working at the novelty shop. I wasn't intending to give in so easily, now. She opened her mouth to protest, then shut it tightly. "I don't have money saved up. Yet," she admitted. "So tell me."

"Nuh-uh." It really wasn't that I got a thrill refusing

her. Here's the thing: Martina was too smart to be spoon-fed. We both knew it. "Use your head," I suggested. "What's magic based on?"

"Misdirection." With a flip, she tossed back her mouse-brown hair. We were back at the elementary level of instruction, here. "I *know* that."

"Right. Misdirection. To create an effect of magic, you have to make your audience believe that their eyes are seeing one thing when really something else entirely is happening. Keep their eyes busy. . . ."

Martina's friend, bored now that the trick was over, wandered over to a rack and began running her fingers through hanging spools of glittery stickers. Martina didn't seem to notice. "And you can do anything you want, yeah, I *know*." She crossed her arms, too, matching my stance. Scary, how she was exactly like me at that age, down to the mule-headedness and the need to know how everything worked. Being a junior Vick was the last fate I'd wish on anyone.

I softened up a little. "Figure it out on your own. Obviously a pencil didn't go through this card," I said, holding it out for examination.

Her little hands turned it over and over again before handing it back. "Obviously," she sniped.

"But a pencil did go through a card. You saw the hole." I held up the ace. "So this is the root of it: how can one thing be in two places at the same time?" She mulled over the question for a few seconds, then shook her head, mouth pursed. It made me impatient when she gave up so easily. "Think about it at home," I suggested. "Because that's the key to the trick. Hey—!"

Have you ever had one of those moments in which you're startled out of what's going on because you've seen something familiar, yet out of place, in the background? Right then, over the rows of novelty pencils and the cartoon lunchboxes and the Magic 8-Balls and all the clothing my store carries, outside among the crowd of people doing their Saturday evening shopping and hanging out, I thought I saw Gio. *That's stupid*, I thought to myself, instantly. *He's volunteering at the old folks' home all evening.* One of the things I learned when I started studying magic is that the brain is a big pattern recognizer; it takes various unrelated things and links them together into something meaningful. Like, it takes the smell of melting cheese and the taste memory of pepperoni grease and the sight of an open delivery box on the counter, and thinks, *Pizza for dinner!* For me, I'd seen some spiky blond hair and a pair of dark eyebrows, a quick shot of a straight-angled nose, a flash of teeth, and I'd thought, *Gio!* But that was crazy. Gio was miles from here. Even if he'd gotten a day off, he would've stopped in to say hello. Besides, what would Gio be doing in a pair of black jeans and a black polo shirt? When it came to his jeans, he was totally in the blue camp.

Mini-Me had been thinking about my question, while my attention wandered. "How can one thing be in two places at the same time," she repeated slowly. Atta girl. She was already trying to puzzle her way through the mystery. She'd get it sooner or later. I flourished the ace in my hand, then folded my fingers around it and twisted my wrist. When I opened it again and showed her the flat of my hand a second later, the card was gone. "Now show me how your palming's going," I said, reaching into my pocket and tossing her a quarter.

Palming is one of those things that every magician has to learn how to do—the earlier the better. I watched as Martina held up the coin between her thumb and forefinger. She'd been practicing, I could tell. Her confidence was better, for one thing, and she mostly looked at me instead of at what she was doing, unlike most beginners. A good sleight of hand artist can make or break an illusion with her eyes, and making the audience feel unwilling to break eye contact was one of the many ways of keeping them distracted from the trick's mechanics. While I watched, Martina passed her free hand over the other, flat and knuckles out, briefly blocking the quarter from sight.

It looked like she hadn't moved a muscle, but when her hand moved down, the coin had vanished. "Good!" The girl let out a quick sigh at my genuine approval. "But don't hold your breath while you're doing it. Loosen up. The only part of your body that should be tense is this one," I told her, flipping over the free hand and pointing to the ball of her thumb. It was clenched slightly—just enough to clutch an edge of the quarter in its fold. To anybody else it would look from the other side as if she couldn't possibly be holding anything, but a good magician would know that this eleven-year-old had pulled off a nearly perfect palm. "You've been practicing in the mirror, haven't you? I can tell. Now do it again, a little faster. You don't want anyone to have the hint of a suspicion that you can pick up a coin that quick—that's it!" I said, when she made the pass again in roughly half the time. She still looked a little anxious, but hey. With practice and experience, that would go away.

I made her run through the routine a few more times while I gave helpful tips. This was exactly the reason I'd been hired. Over the summer, when it became painfully obvious I needed to bring some money into the house, I'd marched right into Novel Tees and told Mr. Schecter he needed to hire me. I had my reasons all lined up: A, I'd hauled Gio there all the time to buy stuff from his shop when we needed equipment for one of the magic shows we'd sometimes do at kids' birthday parties or scout meetings. B, no one in this town could demonstrate the stuff he sold better than me. And C, D, and E, did I need to mention all the money that I'd already brought his way? Heck, I wouldn't have turned me down, either. So although I cashed people out at the front sometimes, helped out with inventory, and did all the things Mr. Schecter expected his other staff to do, what he really wanted was for me to man the counter in the back where he kept the magical gimmicks and equipment, and to lure people into buying it. For me, it was a pretty decent racket, even if it did mean occasionally having to deprive inquisitive little eleven-year-olds of their allowances.

"Think about that Ace of Spades," I called out to Martina when finally she collected her little buddy and reluctantly headed for the exit. "You'll figure it out."

"Oh, I *know* I will," she said, not losing an ounce of

the attitude. Right before she headed out the door and set off the entry beeper, though, she turned and gave me a wave.

Her companion twisted to give me one last look as well. "Is it true she's a witch?"

"Shut *up*," Martina hissed. Then they were gone.

Yeah. Well. I deserved that. All the year before, I'd been so full of myself and my sleight of hand skills that I'd kind of pretended that they weren't tricks and illusions, but real magic. Part of me didn't like to think about that. It hadn't been my finest moment. There was yet another part that bristled whenever it came up, though. If people had kept their eyes open—really open—they wouldn't have fallen for it, would they? Gio hadn't. He'd been the only one to see through to the real me, and now . . . well, I was getting that gooey feeling inside again. I found myself fondling my quartz pendant. Maybe it was better not to think about him at work.

It seemed lately like there were a lot of things it was easier not to think about.

"Oh my God." Oh, creeping crud. Tabitha. I'd managed to forget about her, but now that Martina and company were out of the store, there she was, grinning like a maniac and bouncing back over again. Over her deep purple top she had draped a black Kindergoths T-shirt. "This would look *fantastic* on you. Or on me. Hmmm." She turned to look at herself in the mirror to the counter's side. There was something decidedly different about her that evening. Nothing was really off about her dark brown velvet pull-on pants or the deep purple top she wore, but somehow I'd always pegged Tabitha as a pastels kind of girl. "I bet it would look great on both of us! We could be T-shirt buddies!"

To say I'd rather be dead than caught wearing that thing was putting it mildly. I'd rather be sent to the morgue with embarrassing holes in my undies for all the embalmers to snicker over, then be laid out in my coffin without a stitch of clothing and accidentally have my open casket end up in the funeral home room reserved for the service of Sister Mary Margaret of the Order of the Little Flower. Yeah, a bunch of horrified priests and nuns seeing me starkers would be a *lot* better than being—merely thinking the phrase made my skin crawl—*T-shirt-buddies*—with Tabitha Hunter. I snatched the clothing from her and started to refold it. "Were you here for anything in particular?" I asked her, hoping she'd take the hint.

Instead of realizing she'd long overstayed her welcome like I'd hoped, Little Miss Perfect leaned forward and rested her elbows on the counter. The tips of her long, straight hair barely swept the glass when she rested her chin on her hands. "I'm so bored," she announced. I froze. Was she expecting me to entertain her? If she thought I'd haul out the magician's hat and produce rabbits, she had another think coming. "Don't you ever get tired of, you know, being yourself? Maybe I should get a job. You looked *so cute* with that little girl." Did she really think the only reason I worked was because it was cute? I had to have this job—I wasn't like Gio, who'd been forbidden on penalty of parental flaying from filling out the old W-4s because it might interfere with his studies. I stared at her. Replying would be a sign that I was, you know, invested in the conversation. "She really looked up to you and everything."

"Yeah, well." I slid open the cabinet and moved a few things around, so I could look busy. I'm not one of those people who likes to talk about how wonderful I am. But yeah, I'd been helping Martina along and it showed. She might not ever be a professional magician or anything, but she was really getting off on learning skills that might one day lead to it; she might want to know how things were done right off the bat, but she seemed to realize how much practice and *work* it took to get there. A small part of all that was due to me. So it was kind of hard not to preen a little. "She's the one putting in the sweat," I said, trying to sound like I didn't care. Once I'd slid the cabinet shut and collected the keys, I stepped out from behind the counter and walked to the front of the store. Mr. Schecter was working at the front counter, where he was talking to someone on the phone. I kept an eye out in case he needed me. "Being good at something doesn't come easy."

"Oh, I know!" Tabitha had turned around in place to follow me. "Like in gymnastics. The first time I ever got on the parallel bars I didn't know *what* to do. I kind of hung there like a monkey until the coach finally told me to let someone else have a turn. But then I started practicing on my own and figuring out how to get from one to the other and now I really like it. Like that, right?"

"Yeah," I said. "Like that." Tabitha had never personally been mean to me or my friends, so it was hard for me to work up an active dislike against her. Still, when you're trying to cultivate indifference, it's mighty unfair of someone to roll over and show you a side of their personality you can sympathize with. Unless, of course, she knew exactly what she was doing. Aw, holy heck. I was being unfair. I knew I had a porcupine personality. It had been pointed out to me often enough. Maybe I needed to soften up a little. "I didn't know you did parallel bars," I managed to say. "That's pretty cool."

"You should come watch sometime," she suggested, fiddling with another Kindergoths T-shirt hanging on the rack I leaned against. I was going to have to slap her hands in a minute, I knew. "Hey," she said, changing tone. "Are you and Gio going to Brandon Jerome's party next weekend?"

I'm not sure what it was, exactly, but the way she shifted her weight and avoided looking directly at me when she asked that question made me think that at last we'd gotten down to business. She'd come to nag me at work about a party? Things were indeed getting weird in this town. "I wasn't planning to," I said. "And I don't think Gio knows about it, necessarily."

"Oh, he does." So confident and assured did she sound that I stopped fixing Bates Motel key rings on a spinning rack and stared at her again. "Of course he does. Brandon and Tyler and Clancy invited pretty much anyone who's anyone. And Gio . . ."

Yeah, Gio was pretty much a someone. Me, on the

other hand? Not so much. "He never said anything." I felt a little hurt. Shouldn't my own boyfriend have told me he was invited to a party?

"Maybe he thought you'd say no? I mean, don't get me wrong," she said, hastily trying to cover up the fact that she'd seconds before implied I was a social leper. "I'm sure he'd love it if you went, but you know, people have been *trying* to get you guys to come to stuff and you never do." I covered up my confusion by trying to sort out more name-plated key rings. Turn your back on those things for a minute, and all the Andreas end up in the Timothys. It was totally true that every now and then over the summer, some kid would invite Gio and me to a party or to hang out at the mall, or even once for a day at the Grand Island water park, but whenever Gio had asked if I was interested, I'd answer with a single raised eyebrow. Had he just . . . stopped asking? "I think you should come," she said, picking up one of the Nebraska license plate key rings and fiddling with it. Idly, her fingers searched through the Ts, probably looking for her own name. "It'll be fun. Everyone will be there."

Everyone would be there drinking, I thought to myself. Alcohol had already done enough damage to my family. "Who's everyone?" I asked, not really caring when she began to rattle off a list of names. I was still a little stung at the thought that Gio might be keeping things from me. Not like, actual deep dark secret things. Little things, like party invitations, were bad enough. Isn't that the way bad things started? As tiny oversights? One day you've got a little crack in the ceiling and a few months later the roof's caving in. Did it work that way with secrets? A guy neglects to mention a party or two to the one person he's said again and again means more to him than anything in the world, and then the next thing you know, the two of them have nothing to say to each other? The thought of it chilled me. "Oh, I see," I sighed, when she finished her list. Half-seriously, I said, "It's going to be one of those *Carrie*-style events with every jock, potential prom queen, and A-lister in the school plotting my humiliation. It's all fun and games until someone gets a bucket of pig's blood on her head."

She laughed as if I'd said something outrageous. "Oh, stop! It's a bunch of people hanging out and probably watching videos, that kind of thing! Stop being such an elitist!" Elitist! Me? She had to be kidding. "It's like I said earlier. Sometimes you get bored with yourself and need to step outside for a while. Come to the party! Bring some of your friends. Brie's already supposed to be there. Maybe you could take . . . I don't know." Suddenly she got busy with a hanging display of collectible plush toys, plucking them from their hooks and replacing them until I thought I'd have to grab her by her chunky bead necklace and toss her to the Aeropostale across the way. "Your friend Ray."

"Who?" I asked, totally surprised. Brie I could've understood. Addy, sure. But Ray? Don't get me wrong, I loved Ray. Ray was easily the most creative person I knew, but no sane person would ever describe Ray as a party animal. "No, no, I heard," I told her, when she started to repeat herself. "I'm a little surprised you know Ray, that's all." Quickly my hands went out to straighten the plushies she'd screwed up.

Hurricane Tabitha, who didn't seem to notice that I was trying to clean up the wreckage she left in her path, twisted a Fester Jester in her hands. "Oh, we were in Language Arts together last year. I mean, in the same A.P. class. I didn't sit near him or anything. Gio was in there, too. I . . . well, I kind of thought . . ." Abruptly, I stopped tidying. There weren't any other customers in the store, so Tabitha's voice sounded unnaturally loud even when she mumbled. "He seems kind of, you know. Cool."

She was totally up to something. Once I realized exactly what it was, my eyes narrowed. "Hang on," I said, feeling like I'd gotten a good bang to the head with the stupid stick. "You *like* Ray!" Tabitha's eyes widened in denial, but when she blushed prettily, I knew I was right. The surprise of it made me almost giddy. "Oh my God!"

"You're laughing at me," she accused, more quietly than before. "I thought it would be interesting to get to know him better, that's all."

"No, no, no," I said in a hurry. At any other point in the evening, I would've welcomed Mr. Schecter coming over, staring at me over his half-moon glasses, and giving me a warning about socializing during working hours. I would've *paid* him to do it. Now all I could do was worry he might actually get the notion in his head. Pulling her further back in the store, I helped myself to a stack of T-shirts that I began to sort on the magic equipment counter, trying to appear busy. The idea of anyone having a hot pants explosion for Ray was . . . well, it was something I'd never really considered before, for so standoffish a person. Then again, he had been awfully smooth-acting in the hallway earlier that week. "So tell me. You two were in class together? And what happened?"

I'd never sounded so girly before in my life. Soon I'd be pulling my hair back from my face and reading the boys-and-beauty-tips magazines at the Pharm-A-Copia and from there it'd be a slippery slope to comparing lipsticks with the other fembots in the restroom between classes. Tabitha didn't seem to notice anything out of the ordinary, however. "Well," she said, wearing the look of relief that comes with having someone to confide in. "At the beginning of the year, Ray sat at the far left of the room, three seats from the front, and I sat three rows from the right and two seats from the back, and then after the holiday break he moved to the second row from the left, four seats back, and so I told Frankie Pescatori that I was having trouble seeing the board, so she swapped seats with me so that I was *four* rows from the left and *four* seats from the. . . ."

Oh my God, if this is what girly-girls talked like when they got together, I was going to have to give them a lot more credit than I ever had. My freakin' head felt like it might explode. "Yeah, so you moved closer," I said, hurrying along her lesson in the Geography of Love.

"Right," she said, pleased I got the point. No more fiddling with the merchandise now, I noticed; she was all about the story. "Then one day, Mr. Camm had Ray read one of his poems out loud in class." Back in the day when my little group had been the chunks of limburger among the perfect, square Kraft-processed American cheese food slices, Ray had actually been invited to read one of his poems at the dedication of the new city hall. No one gave a flying leap at a rolling doughnut about us then—so why the interest now? Maybe it was wrong of me to be so suspicious of Tabitha. She seemed totally sincere as she talked. "It was called 'House of Solitude.' And it was about this girl who built a brick wall around her so she wouldn't have to look at the ugliness of the world outside . . . oh, it was really beautiful. It really got to me."

Was she going to cry? Was I going to have to offer her a Kleenex? Was I going to have to—oh, no. Oh, no! Was I going to have to *hug* her? No, my little Elizabeth Barrett Browning was okay. Only a momentary sniffle. "Yeah, Ray's a good poet. I mean, the stuff I've read, anyway. He doesn't mention his poetry often, though."

"I don't suppose he's ever . . ." Before finishing her thought, Tabitha shook her head and looked away. I didn't have to be the most tuned-in of girls to know the one way that sentence could end: *I don't suppose he's ever mentioned me?*

"Ray's a pretty private person," I said carefully. I didn't want to tramp on Tabitha's feelings, for some reason. She had never been a part of the Hair Club for Harpies that had made our lives unbearable the year before. Maybe there's something about having someone of your own that makes you want other people to be happy, too. But mostly I didn't want Ray hurt. There were reasons that other kids picked on him.

"You know Ray's different, right?" Part of me felt horrible at asking the question, like I was talking about one of my friends behind his back. It was no big secret, but I still felt invasive. "I mean, he's not like other guys?"

"I know he writes the most beautiful poetry," she said, gooney-eyed.

Oh, crud. She simply wasn't getting it. I hated having to spell it out for her, but if I didn't and she made a play for Ray and found out later, she'd be freaked. And if Tabitha left Ray hurt when she ran away, well, all I could say was that I'd have to show her what pain really felt like. "No," I told her, trying to find a tactful way to come up with the words. "I'm saying . . . okay. You know that on the outside, Ray might look like any other guy, but underneath . . ."

"He's really sensitive, you mean." Tabitha nodded as if she got it.

No, that wasn't what I meant at all! I could've growled with frustration. "What I'm trying to say is, you know that Ray has different *parts* than other guys, right?"

There. I couldn't get any more blunt than that. For a second, I thought that I'd ripped the blinders from Tabitha's little Clearasil-complected face. At best, she'd stammer out a denial, then realize I wasn't joking and make some polite excuse and disappear from my life forever—and at worst, she'd run out screaming into the mall and collide with a sample-carrying cheese-on-a-stick employee and put her eye out. At long last she put her hands on her hips and tilted her head. Here came the blunt denial. "Oh my God," she said, laughing. I knew it! She thought I was kidding her! "You are so *cute*. The word is *transgendered*."

My skin felt a little flushed. Was I red? Maybe I was. "Um, yeah," I said, wishing I could bury my flaming face in a cool, cool vat of dry ice. "That's the word all right."

"Of course I know that. Everyone knows that," Tabitha informed me, arms crossed. Now I felt like the one who should run from the store. When you live with a friend's idiosyncrasies for so long, you tend not to notice them anymore. Like everyone in my formerly little group, I thought of Ray as one of the boys. And he looked so much like a genuine, hundred-percent-down-to-the-sideburns-and-baby-hair-mustache male that I could see someone being surprised to find out otherwise. But no, Tabitha was totally my superior at that moment, and I looked like the utter dork that I was. Then she gasped a little. "Oh!" she said, clutching her chest. "You think—! No, it's not like I want to . . . oh no," she said, shaking her head with vigor. "I'm not looking for that from him!"

I'm not sure which of us was more flustered right then. She had turned as plum red as I felt. "Yeah, I know!" I told her, totally lying through my teeth. What was I supposed to think? She was the one who'd been wanting to be someone else for a change! "I wasn't saying you did!"

"I wanted to get to know him better, that's all!"

"Okay, okay, I didn't think anything different," I repeated, looking toward the front of the store to see if Mr. Schecter had overheard. One of our shrieks of protest must have reached his ears, because he was looking right at me. He didn't seem mad that I was talking, though; he only gestured to me with two hairy-knuckled fingers. "Sheesh."

She calmed down a little and followed me as I made my way up to the front of the store, weaving through the buttloads of crap we marked at forty percent over cost and sold to an unsuspecting public. "It's that I think he's really talented," she explained to me. "And a cool guy. And of course I know about the transgendered thing. That's what makes Ray, Ray, isn't it?" When I dodged around the bin of band posters that were some of the store's biggest sellers and stood in front of Mr. Schecter, she was still jabbering. "It really doesn't matter if a guy doesn't have all the parts a guy has, when there's no way I'm going to be there at night when his pants hit the floor. Right?"

The last question was addressed more to Mr. Schecter than anyone else. Poor old guy. He rubbed his hand over his ear (what is it about guys over forty suddenly sprouting hair from any square inch of skin not already totally covered with fur? The day that Gio started growing fleece on his back or ears was the day that I'd buy a pair of clipping shears) and stared at her over the tops of his glasses. "I was going to get some water from the store," he said to me, unable to tear his eyes away from Tabitha. "Perhaps I could get you an Icee?"

What a boss! He would have treated me, too, but I shook my head. I didn't want to be anyone's charity case. "No thanks. I'll watch the counter while you're gone. My friend's leaving in a minute."

I cringed inside when I saw how Tabitha's posture

straightened at the words *my friend*. Mr. Schecter, though, pushed his thick frames up his nose and, with his eyebrows raised, smiled and said, "No hurry. No hurry at all."

Tabitha waited until he was nearly through the door before chirping out, "Bye!" Mr. Schecter nearly collided into a woman with a double-stroller when he turned around to take a last look at my guy-parts-lovin' acquaintance. "He's so *nice*," she finally declared. "It must be really nice to work for someone who's so nice."

"Yeah, it's, um, nice," I said lamely, assuming my position behind the counter.

And still, Tabitha made no signs of leaving. "I really should get a job. I bet you have all kinds of extra money for CDs and stuff. Plus you get to meet all kinds of fun people!"

"That's not why I have a job," I said, feeling a stab of annoyance at her words.

Not that it was any of her business, but I hadn't bought a CD in months and months. And I could do without any of the "fun" people who streamed into the store expecting my immediate and unwavering attention. "I still think it would be a blast," she sighed. "So," she said, changing topics. "You'll ask him?"

"Who?"

"Ray!" she said, laughing at silly ol' me for not being able to read her mind. "To the party!"

"Rude! I can't ask Ray to someone else's party!" I told her, wishing I was anywhere else but there.

"Sure you can. It's not *that* kind of party. I'll make it good with Brandon, don't worry. So?"

She looked at me with such imploring eyes that I wanted to duck behind the counter and hold my breath until she went away. "I don't know if I'm going, myself!"

"Oh of course you are, you big silly!" she giggled again. "You and Gio both."

There are a lot of insects, especially in the summertime, that never seem to get the point you don't want them hovering around you, buzzing and flapping. There's plenty of other space in the universe they could be occupying, but no. There they are, right in your face, doing their insect-y thing. Tabitha was one of those bugs. No matter how much I swatted or pretended she wasn't there, she had no intention of going away. Could it be the scent of my shampoo? That always seemed to attract wasps, for some reason. "I'll see what I can do."

"Oh, come on. That means no. Say yes."

Oh, poop. She'd nailed me—I had meant no. "I will do my best. Honestly," I added, looking her up and down. There really was something decidedly different about her appearance. "I'll talk to Gio and if he wants to go, I'll tell Ray. . . ."

I couldn't finish the sentence. Once again while my mouth was on autopilot, my brain had gone running leaps and bounds ahead of it. Although I really wasn't paying attention to anything more than Tabitha's heart-shaped little face, out in the mall, on the fringes of my vision, I saw that familiar face again, walking in the direction of the food court, the opposite of the first time. *Hey look! It's Gio!,* my brain told me.

Tabitha kept talking while I stepped out from behind the register and ran for the door. "You'll tell Ray to come? Only, okay, don't tell him *I* wanted him to come. I don't want to look like, you know, a total spaz or anything. Vick?"

"Is that Gio?" I asked, more to myself than anything. The figure I'd seen was the same as before, when I'd been talking to Martina, down to the black jeans and the black shirt. He seemed to be with some girl, similarly dressed. But all I could really see of the guy at that point was the back of his head, and he'd moments before covered that with a black baseball cap. A baseball cap? Come on. Eighty-five percent of the guys at Millard Fillmore spent their free time curling their caps in coffee cups so they could achieve the perfect inward curve of the brim that bestowed some kind of weird cool status known only among members of the XY chromosome tribe, but that wasn't Gio. For one thing, he was so vain about that spiky 'do of his. A cap would only crush the peaks.

"Where?" Tabitha stood beside me, looking out at the evening crowds. Too many people were hauling their purchases to their cars before the mall closed, and she hadn't seen the guy I had. "And he didn't stop to see you? Rude!"

I couldn't leave the shop. With Mr. Schecter gone for the next few minutes, I was the only person there. "It wasn't him," I told her, hauling myself back in. The guy in black was long gone now, anyway. "My mistake."

All I'd seen was some other kid about Gio's height and build, with Gio's shade of blond hair. And Gio's walk, halfway between a swagger and a stroll. It was like the most elementary sleight of hand—my eye had been tricked into seeing what it wanted to see, and after a long evening at work, what I wanted to see most was the face of the guy who made me light up from the inside, every time he came near.

And when I told him about it next time I saw him, we'd have a good laugh about it, right?

Right? Right? Anybody?

Yeah, I didn't think so. It's criminal, what a bad track record I have for predicting the future.

CHAPTER FOUR

You know what I liked best about Gio? From time to time, when he knew I was looking, he would turn his head in my direction and smile. Most of the time, he didn't have a reason for doing it. He wouldn't even have anything to say, necessarily. We'd be watching television, or playing one of his videogames, or studying at the branch library and out of nowhere I'd get a flash of those straight, white teeth. Every single time I'd try to imagine what had prompted that simple kindness a delicious shiver would run up my spine.

I really like that you're here, that smile seemed to say. *Thank you for being with me.*

What girl who hadn't been drinking the Kookoo-Cola wouldn't love that? When Gio let loose one of those handsome grins over his shoulder, right at the start of the cafeteria line the following Monday, I nearly melted. When it happened, half of me always wanted to remind myself that only stupid girls lost their heads over a pretty sexy look from a pretty sexy guy. The other half wanted to be as stupid as stupid could be. For a moment I forgot to pick up a tray from the stack. "I was kind of hoping we could eat outside today. On one of the benches near Pop Alley," I told him, feeling suddenly shy. I'd had to work all Sunday afternoon, and he was too pooped from the volunteer thing all weekend to meet the night before. We'd talked a little that morning at our lockers, but I craved a little bit of private time.

"It's all of fifty degrees out," he said.

I was about to explain when out of nowhere, a melon-shaped head set atop a small and wiry body popped up. "If you need help keeping warm, baby, you know I'm your man."

"Tony, scram!" I groaned. Why was I the victim of a perpetual series of bad jokes? Was I jinxed? "I meant you and me," I said to Gio. "Us. By ourselves."

We were holding up the line. A couple of impatient people passed by, the corners of their trays digging into my back as they inched around. Gio gave Tony a jerk of the head. With a visible shrug of disappointment, the kid detoured around the poor schmoes like me waiting for a hot lunch, and headed for the exit. Why didn't he obey *me* that quickly? "Yeah, sure," he said, once we were kinda-sorta alone. "Anything you want. You getting a hot lunch today?" he asked, nodding at the tray and bundle of plastic utensils I'd collected. "I was going to pick up an orange juice, but I'll walk through the line with you, if you want."

"No!" Cheese on crackers, did he see how much I panicked at that suggestion? I tried to play it cool and ignore the fact that not only were my armpits a little less fresh than moments before, but I'd also come close to rupturing my boyfriend's eardrums by shriek-ing at dog-whistle frequencies. "I mean, you should get your juice and go find us a table outside before they fill up, right?"

"Fill up? It's too cold!" he said mildly. "Besides, I like spending time with you."

Now he was making me feel worse for pushing him away, but the last thing I wanted was for him to be with me when I reached the line's end. All my friends were devotees of the sack lunch; since the beginning of the year I'd managed to avoid having any of them present at the dreaded moment of truth by the cash register. I didn't want to start the afternoon with a grand unveiling. "Oh, please. I got up late and forgot to get anything out of the fridge. It'll take a couple of seconds to grab some stuff and I'll be right there. It kind of smells in here, anyway." I gave him a little smile to let him know it was okay. "Go on."

"Sure." It didn't take much imagination to see that he was relieved not to have to stand in the steamy tunnel of bad odors. "Don't take too long, though."

The peck on the cheek he gave me would have been incentive enough to make me finish quickly. I watched as he dove into the cooler and emerged with a bottle of juice, then took the same route around the tray-bearers that Tony had a couple of minutes earlier.

I hated to think it, but I was glad he was gone.

"That was kinda sweet." When I turned around, I had to crane my neck back to see who was address-ing me. My first impression was of a torpedo, like I'd seen on the old-fashioned late-night movies. But no, it was just Tyler Woodwell—six feet and one inch of lean dopiness garnished with the tight gray wool cap that always seemed to cover the top of his head. He grinned at me like the big halfwit he was.

I toughened up my exterior so he wouldn't be able to see my embarrassment. "It's called kissing. Among higher-order primates it's a show of affection." I snatched a carton of milk from the cooler and slammed my tray down on the metal railing. The tired-looking woman hovering over the steam trays asked her daily question. I pointed to the meat patties in gravy, the artificial mashed potatoes, and then with a little reluctance at the succotash. "Maybe one of these days, when your *cojones* drop, you'll understand how grown-up boys feel for girls."

"Ouch!" Tyler mimed shaking his hand like I'd nipped the fingers in a closing car door. "Dial it down a few notches, Marotti. I wasn't mocking you. I was saying it was sweet, that's all." Over the countertop, the cafeteria lady held out to him a nearly identical plate of glop. He studied it for a quick second, then said, "Stop doing that."

I hadn't been looking his way, so I wasn't sure if he meant to address me. "Stop what?" I asked, turning around.

"That thing you do whenever I'm around." He nodded to let me know the kids in front had moved on. I slid my tray in the direction of the desserts. "The one where you act like I'm going to steal candy from your trick-or-treat bag."

"I don't know what you're talking about," I said loftily. "I don't like candy." I pretended to study the desserts while I tried to rally. "I don't do a thing."

"You do a thing," he said. "You clench."

Outraged, my jaw dropped. "I do not clench!"

Tyler nodded. "You clench." His quick demonstration resembled constipation. What a boob! I should know better than anyone if there's clenching going on. "Blue Jell-O or green Jell-O?"

"What?" When he gestured toward the cling-wrapped bowls of wobbling ick, I grabbed a covered plate of two small oatmeal cookies, dropped it onto my tray, and slid ahead.

And still he was talking. "I like the blue Jell-O, myself. Green, orange, red—you can almost believe that they might have once come from a fruit. Or might have been in the general vicinity of a fruit, even. Blue, though? Bears absolutely no relationship at all to anything you can buy at a grocery store. I mean, who's ever heard of blue food?"

"Blueberries?" I countered. I had no idea what he was going on about.

"Have you ever looked at a blueberry, though? Not blue at all. More purple, really, or a dark navy."

"Blue M&M's?"

Usually, when I delivered a sentence in my lowest voice and accompanied it with my raised eyebrow, people knew not to push my buttons. Not Tyler, though. He helped himself to the napkins and straws while we waited to have the cashier check us out. "Excellent food product, and one hundred percent artificial," he said. "See what I mean? So you know blue Jell-O's *got* to be good, being man-made and all." When I didn't say anything, he shut up for a minute. I was hoping that would be the end of it, but he yapped on. "So how'd you do on the social studies test?"

I turned once more and scrutinized him, unleashing the trademarked Vick Marotti What Smells So Bad In Here Oh Yes It Must Be You Stare Of Death. Everyone fears the V.M.W.S.S.B.I.H.O.Y.I.M.B.Y.S.O.D. One flash of the V.M.W.S.S.B.I.H.O.Y.I.M.B.Y.S.O.D. could dry up canker sores, small ponds, and the gross national product of really tiny countries. As a matter of fact, the kid immediately behind Tyler who had poked his head around impatiently to see what was holding up the line, immediately cringed back into place.

One person was totally clueless about the look's significance, though. "See, that's what I'm talking about. You clench." I was about to protest, but Tyler added, "What did I ever do to you?"

"Oh!" He was going to go there, was he? Well, fine, we'd go there. "What did you ever do to me? How about last year when you and your buddies tied me up and threw me into the band closet? Hmmm? What about that?"

He matched my crossed arms and cocked head. "I wasn't there."

"Oh yes, you . . ." Oh, no, he hadn't been, I remembered suddenly. There had been plenty of the school's slimy underside present at that spectacular stunt, an illusion Gio and I had intended to catapult me into legendary status—the greatest disappearing act of all time. "Oh."

"Yeah, actually, it seems to me that people said Gio was the guy who actually kind of egged people into doing it." Well, of course he had. It was before we were officially an item, when people didn't know that we liked each other. Gio had set it up so it would look like I'd been attacked, when really the moment I was in that band closet, I had scampered up into the crawl space above the ceiling and over to the janitor's closet across the hall. Tyler gave me a curious glance. "And you're pretty friendly with him now."

"That's different," I said.

I might've explained why, too, only he kept running his mouth. "As a matter of fact, the *reason* I wasn't around for that was because you'd broken my leg."

"That," I said, sliding a little closer to the cashier, "was a coincidence."

"According to popular legend, you laid a curse on me and said something bad was going to happen. Then a week later I broke my leg in three places and haven't played ball since. I remember being in physical therapy that day. Because of you. But you don't see me holding a grudge." He bared his teeth at me in a smile, as if to prove the point.

A little head poked around Tyler's midsection. It was the nameless freshman behind him again. "Aren't you going to move?" he whined.

"Are you *really* that anxious to eat the Salisbury steak? There's dog meat in it, you know," I snapped at the kid, though I knew it was the kind of thing that could get me in trouble with the Oostermonster.

"Go on around," Tyler told the boy, who scurried past with his head down. "She's counting carbs. Makes her ornery."

"I guess," I heard the kid mutter.

"That wasn't a real curse I laid on you," I informed

Tyler. Being this honest was painful. My friends might know that my witchy ways had been nothing but parlor tricks, but the rest of the school? So long as they thought I was reformed, I'd let them have their own theories. "If you're really so stupid to think that one person can curse another . . ."

"I know it wasn't real." I was so surprised at his reply that I could only stare at him in disbelief. "Unless you stood behind me and shoved when I stepped on my kid sister's skateboard and went slamming down the stairs. I never told anyone the accident was your fault. Everyone else made that assumption."

I gave him a grudging look. Maybe Tyler had more on the ball than I'd originally thought. His social studies notes hadn't been half bad, either. We were coming closer to the cashier, now. In fact, the kid in front of me was scooping up his tray and heading off into the pandemonium of the lunchroom. Right at that moment, as I reached for the wallet I kept stuffed in the pocket of my ratty cargos, I felt a sudden moment of panic. "You go around," I told Tyler. He raised his eyebrows so that they nearly scraped the rim of his wool cap. "Go, already!" I commanded.

"All right, all right," he muttered, picking up his tray and moving to the head of the line. "Jeez, you try to be friendly to someone. . . ."

"I need to get out my money." He'd made me feel vaguely guilty. I knew I could be abrupt. After being pushed-around Vickie for so long, I'd developed a spiky exterior to protect myself. Letting go of it wasn't proving as easy as I hoped. "Just . . . go ahead."

He didn't need my encouragement. He was already

giving the cashier a grimy wad of cash, his attention elsewhere. That was fine with me. I really didn't need him seeing what I was pulling out from the back slot of my wallet, hidden away where no one could see. The blue-rimmed flimsy card tucked there was my secret shame, the symbol of everything that had gone wrong in the last three months. I palmed it so neither Tyler nor the guy behind me could see.

When I looked up, Tyler stood beyond the cashier, waiting. "Go on," I said, trying not to sound too loud or desperate. "Don't wait. Enjoy your blue Jell-O." He didn't move. "Buh-bye!" He shook his head, turned, and walked through the doorway. At last!

Melba, the cashier, nodded at me when I slipped her the plastic card; she scanned it, nodded, and let me go. Although she and I had been through the same transaction every day for weeks, and although she'd never once done anything other than smile at me, I never walked away from her station with my head held high. Like some kind of criminal fleeing the scene of the crime, I grabbed my tray, mumbled a shamed thank you, and fled toward the outside doors. It was stupid. At heart I knew I wasn't the only kid receiving free lunches out of Uncle Sam's pocket. There had to be plenty of us in the school. The simple fact was that I wished like hell my dad and I weren't so badly off that I had to be one of them. I wished he hadn't lost his job, or that he'd find another. I wished . . . I wished a lot of stuff.

Despite the fact it was a little cool, the fresh air felt great. The quiet was even better. Beyond the cafeteria's rear lay a pathway leading to the student parking lot, where a corrugated metal roof protected a bunch of soda machines. Everybody always called it Pop Alley, and it was kind of a pity that it had a reputation for being where the rougher kids hung out, because past where the hulking machines whirred, out on the grass sat a few picnic tables. Gio had taken the one closest to the sidewalk and started to dig into his lunch. "Hey," he said, sounding happy to see me. "Are you going to be warm enough?"

"Sure," I said, eyeing the array of small plastic containers sitting in front of him. Gio's mom surely knew how to pack a lunch for her growing boy. A small salad with some kind of creamy white dressing sat open to his right, while his abandoned fork had been speared front-and-center into what looked like a hamburger patty without a bun, smothered in ketchup—the kind of patty I could see his mom making from a pile of meat and breadcrumbs and spices and onions and his dad cooking on the stainless steel grill decorating their patio. Gio grinned at me as his tongue darted out to catch a dribble of the red goop from the back of his plastic knife. "Isn't that gross cold?"

"Nah. Leftovers are always good cold." He laid the knife on top of a still-sealed container that I could see held a slice of apple pie. It might not have been homemade, but pie bought from the supermarket freezer section and heated up in an oven was a sight more homemade than anything I'd eaten recently. He gestured to my tray as I settled it on the table. "Isn't that gross at any temperature?"

The less said about my lunch, the better. I used the

bottom of my knife to flick a cigarette butt from the bench where I wanted to sit. I wasn't going to be using the knife, anyway. The Salisbury steak was so soft and gloppy that one of Gio's senior citizens could have eaten it without dentures. "I miss you!" I told him, finally settling down.

His hand reached out to cover mine. "I know. I miss you too. It's not like it was over the summer. But it's only a few more weeks."

That wasn't good enough for me, somehow. "And then it'll be Christmas and you'll be too busy with . . . I don't know, tree-chopping and pig roasts and figgy pudding. . . ."

"Figgy pudding?" he asked, with a cackle, having another go at his hamburger patty. "Who do you think I am, Ebenezer Scrooge?"

I was too far gone in my forecast of misery to care. "And then it'll be spring and you'll be too busy with graduation stuff, and then summer you'll be getting ready to go away to school, and after that I'll never see you again." He laughed at me. I really couldn't mind much. "Fine, I know I sound melodramatic, but it's all true, and you know it." Funny that although we were sitting outside in the sun, I felt black and miserable inside. Yet the nights were getting colder and colder that time of autumn, and the sunshine seemed a little tentative and wan, so maybe my mood and the weather weren't that dissimilar. "Where are you going to end up applying, anyway?"

"Duke," he said, spearing some of the salad. He munched on it before he continued. "Because my dad went there and he wants me to go. Stanford.

University of Michigan is my top choice, if I get in. Oh, and University of New Mexico. Maybe. I haven't decided on that one yet."

My stomach felt hollow. He sounded happy enough as he told me his plans, but every word nauseated me. Part of that, of course, might have been the Salisbury steak I tried to wolf down while he spoke. "So basically, East Coast, West Coast, and out in the middle of the desert. As far away as you can get from here as possible." *And from me*, I thought to myself. *As far away from me.*

He paused in midbite. "Hello? When did you join the drama club? University of Michigan is not that far." I turned my head so he wouldn't see how I was having to clench my jaw to keep from showing any weakness. "And it's not true I'd never see you again."

"Oh yeah, during breaks," I said, trying to keep it light, but feeling more bitter than coffee. "That'll be fun."

He put his food down and reached out for me, taking my chin in his soft hand and gently pulling it until I looked at him again. "You could always go to my college after you graduate." He waited for a reaction. None came. To that kind of statement, none ever would. "It's a year, Vick. You can wait a year." He pulled the pendant he'd given me from beneath my jacket, letting its chain run through his fingers.

Gio was a dreamer, I realized right then. A lover of tidy, happy endings. He always thought he could have anything, where I constantly worried about losing it all. I rested my head on my hand and let my eyes wander over that handsome face, those pouty lips, that cute little nose, the hair that with a little help from some styling mud seemed to defy gravity. "I can wait a year," I told him, because I knew he wanted to hear me say the words. "Sure." I smiled to let him know that everything was okay.

The truth, though? I would never be at college with my sweet Gio. My dad and I could barely afford the rent on our house. We didn't eat out. We didn't stay up late with Thai takeout and watch *I Love Lucy*, the way we used to. After he'd been laid off over the summer and could only find a half-time security guard post, I'd gone out and gotten a part-time job of my own so I wouldn't have to see him live on a diet of peanut butter sandwiches for my sake—and also so I wouldn't have to watch him sitting on the living room sofa for hours, feeling like a failure. I hadn't discussed it with him. We didn't talk about things like that. I'd simply gone out and done it.

College in my future? How? With whose grades? With what money?

How could I wait a year when I wasn't sure from day to day if I'd wake up one morning and find my dad packing our suitcases, ready to hare off some-where else? We'd moved with less warning. Each time he'd landed a worse job in a worse town. I'd never complained, though I wanted to now. I thought I'd found something real here. Something that might last.

Nothing good really lasts, does it? After my mom's accident, again and again I'd watched everything good fall to pieces. Why should now be any different?

I didn't say a word, though. I hadn't meant to come

out here in the sunshine and be Gio's personal little thundercloud. And let's get real: Did I really think he'd give up the shot to attend a fantastic college for me? Nuh-uh. I choked down all the doubts and fears I felt at that moment, wrapped it up in the black uncertainty I didn't want to think about, and hid the heavy bundle somewhere deep, deep inside where it wouldn't show.

It must have worked, because when Gio looked up at me with his brown, puppy-dog eyes, they glowed. "Sure," I repeated with more enthusiasm. "Absolutely." Why bring him down with me? It didn't make any sense. "You know what's weird?" I said, trying to lighten the mood. He shook his head. "Actually having a conversation with you, without Little Tony popping up between us."

I got a laugh at that. "He's a good kid!"

"I know he's a good kid! But that good kid is always showing up when you least want."

"Just ignore him," Gio advised.

"How can I ignore him when he's always there when I need to . . . you know. Kiss you?"

Gio looked thoughtful. I could tell by the way his lips twitched that he planned to make a joke. "I seem to recall that when I was dog-sitting the golden retriever from next door, you wouldn't kiss me in front of it, either."

"Of course not! That's creepy!" I was joking right back, but not entirely. That dog had examined us like it was writing an article on the mating habits of the adolescent human for *Pooch Psychiatry Quarterly.* Plus I'd seen a documentary on reincarnation that week. What if the dog had been someone I knew in a previous life? Like some dead relative? Or the minister who baptized me? "What'd you do to get Tony to keep away? Threaten to beat him up?"

"No," he said, managing to recap with a single word all the *Violence isn't the answer!* lectures I'd ever received from the Oostermonster. Then, grudgingly, he admitted, "I told him I'd give him a ride home in the Mustang."

His head jerked in the direction of the student parking lot, where at the back end, in an empty section, sat his precious 2003 reef blue Mustang. He'd saved up all his birthday and Christmas presents for three years to buy that thing. Boys and their toys! "Man, you always park so far away," I commented, thinking of the dozens of yards between his car and the others. "I thought the point of having wheels was so that you didn't have to walk miles to school."

"So funny I forgot to laugh," he said, reaching across the table to swat the air in front of my face. He sat back, popped the top off of his slice of pie, and began shoveling it in his mouth. "If I park my baby away from everyone, no one can scratch up my paint job," he explained through a mouth full of apple filling.

"Your *baby!*" I'd always known there was some weird thing with guys and cars, but never before had I been forced to see it up close and personal. In a goofy way, it was kind of cute. "You like that car more than you like me," I told him, solely so I could have the pleasure of him looking into my eyes and denying it.

He patted the seat next to him, to tell me to come over. "I don't like anything the way I like you." Then he proved it. As much as you can prove that kind of thing outside the back entrance of a school where anyone could be watching out the windows. But as far as proving went? It was pretty good.

Yeah. If there's anything I'd learned in the last half year, it was that not all boys were really so bad, after all. Having Gio's arms around me, even for a minute, erased everything that was bad in the world. He made me feel protected. If I ever lost that feeling, I didn't know what I'd do.

It wasn't until we had finally separated and collected our lunches—me stuffing the dry cafeteria cookies in my pocket for later and picking up my empty tray, Gio snapping his Tupperware tops and burping them—that we talked again. "This was nice," I said, smiling almost shyly. Weird, how he could make me feel almost bashful. "We ought to do this more often."

"I was thinking the same thing," he said, arm around my shoulders as we walked from the table across the grass.

When our heels hit the pavement, I felt a sinking sensation. This moment grabbed between fourth and fifth periods had been the longest we'd spent together in two weeks. And who knew when I'd see him again? "There's this party, Saturday," I said, trying to sound offhanded about it.

"Yeah, Brandon Jerome's." Gio's body beneath his plaid shirt, where it rested against my back, was all the warmth I'd ever need. "He told me. Said we should come. What—wait a minute." He pulled away and looked at me in astonishment. "You didn't want to *go*, did you?"

"No!" I exclaimed, scornful. After a second, I reconsidered. "Did you?"

"Did you?" he asked, seeming doubtful. "I mean, we could, but I didn't think you'd want to." Oh, creeping crud. Tabitha had been right. Or was there another reason he hadn't wanted to invite me along? That crowd was prettier and better dressed and were able to bring their own lunches in neat little plastic receptacles. I didn't fit in with them. I never had. I never would. More than ever before, right then I felt like Gio might be editing me out of parts of his life. That realization very nearly made me stop walking. "We can talk about it later this week," he suggested. "See if you feel like it."

"I think we should go." The words tasted like bitter medicine, but sometimes medicine was what you needed to make things better, right? "Maybe it'd be fun. You don't have to let Brandon know?"

"It's not that kind of party." I wasn't totally naïve. I didn't think it was going to be Twister and chocolate milk and that then we'd all crowd around the TV and guess along with *The Price Is Right*. "I'll see if I have to work that night. I mean, volunteer."

The whole party discussion had brought up another train of thought. "You know Tabitha Hunter?" I asked. He nodded. "She visited me at work the other night."

"Oh yeah?" He tossed his can in the recycle bin as

we walked past the soda machines. "She seems like a pretty okay person."

I wasn't ready to commit to so wild a concept yet, but I nodded. "It was kind of funny," I said, sounding casual. "We kind of thought we saw you out in the mall at one point."

"What time?" Wait a minute. What kind of question was that? Wasn't he supposed to say, *Of course you didn't* or *Don't be silly?* Not, *What time?*

"After eight-thirty." I studied him closely. I wasn't suspicious, exactly. I trusted Gio. Something in his voice, though, had set me on edge.

"I was at the senior center," he finally said. Then he smiled at me as he held open the door. "Aren't you coming in?"

"No," I said. "Not yet. I'll . . . I'll see you later." A quick peck on my lips and he was gone, back into the loud and crazy world I couldn't bear to rejoin quite yet.

Had my voice sounded weak, to his ears? Had he noticed anything unusual in my reaction? Because I was stunned. Absolutely stunned. When I'd first met Gio and realized he was as into stage magic as I, I'd discovered something about him really quickly: He was a lousy magician. He didn't practice as much as he should have to make every illusion look effortless. Every magic trick is pretty much a lie, really—the magician's feeding the audience one story he hopes they'll buy while really he's doing something else entirely.

Gio was a very bad liar. Before I started teaching

him exactly the same way I was trying to teach Martina, he'd made every trick look like hard, hard work when it should have seemed effortless. His biggest weakness always had been his eyes. They would follow his hands everywhere, giving away his secrets when they should have been charming and sincere.

When Gio had told me that he'd been at the senior center, I didn't believe his eyes. If he had laughed it off or called me a goof, or acted only mildly interested in the way he would when I told him one of my tedious dreams from the night before, I would have accompanied him into the cafeteria without any reservations.

However, everything about his reaction set off every alarm in my brain. He'd lied. I knew it. I couldn't prove it. It might not even have anything to do with his near-twin I'd seen Saturday night. Gio had lied to me, plain and simple. In those last few seconds we'd been together, all the colors of the rainbow had vanished. Although it was still sunny, I'd turned gray and gloomy. The prism had fractured.

What was I going to do now?

The raucous noise of the lunchroom when I slammed my way through the doorway suited my mood—loud, crazy, and unpredictable. I'd intended to push my way through the throng and go hide in a restroom stall until the bell rang. My head throbbed. I scarcely noticed at first when, from out of the crowd, a hand reached out and grabbed my wrist. "Hey," I heard someone say. "Vick."

"Let *go*," I yelled, wrenching my arm free with such force that I accidentally gave myself a wrist burn. I didn't care. The red-hot pain gave me something concrete to focus on. When I looked up—and I had to look up, because the boy who'd grabbed me was so tall—I groaned. It was my wool-capped nemesis, Tyler. "What do you *want?*" I snarled.

"I didn't mean to hurt—I mean . . ." Something in the way I squared off with him, jaw set, eyes blazing, must have warned him that I was not in a mood to be jerked around. "I only wanted to talk for a sec. You seemed kind of embarrassed back there, and . . ."

"What do we have to talk about?" I sounded furious, but though my words flew out like bullets, I knew they weren't aimed at him. Then again, maybe they were. What, had he been spying on the two of us out at the picnic tables? How did he know I was embarrassed? "Just get out of my way."

My escape was arrested by his next words. "Listen. I saw your free lunch card. I only wanted to tell you—"

He didn't get to finish the sentence. The red-hot ball of fire that had been building inside me suddenly exploded. I grabbed a handful of his shirt and yanked him forward. Startled at my strength, he gasped. Fine. That was all I intended. Did he really think a small chick like me could beat him up? Unlikely. While I still had the advantage of surprise, I growled, "Not another word, Woodwell! And if you ever, *ever* tell anyone . . . !"

"Ahem," I heard from behind me. Exactly like that—not a clearing of the throat. Someone actually saying the word *ahem*. Only one person in the school would ever, ever do that. I froze, Tyler's shirt still clutched in my fist, and turned slowly. The Ooster-monster stood immediately to my rear, arms crossed, the mole on her lip quivering. "Vickie, dear. Join me for a little chat in my office."

Holy cannoli! Maybe after all those hexes I'd pretended to cast on people the year before, some of them were coming back to haunt me. I *was* jinxed, after all.

CHAPTER FIVE

I know it's horrible to browse through other people's glove compartments uninvited. It's nearly as bad as being invited to someone's house for dinner, going to the bathroom, and pawing through your host's medicine cabinet. Nosy, nosy, nosy. Of course, when your boyfriend's mother walks in (without knocking, thank you very much!) and catches you with the cabinet door open and your nose investigating her Oil of Olay, that's probably worst of all. I speak from personal experience.

Somehow, though, I didn't think that at the rocket speed we were going we'd have a problem with parental units suddenly appearing. I was a little surprised, though, to find no less than six full-sized Payday candy bars lying atop the maps and the car manual. "Does your mom like salted peanuts and nougat a lot?" I asked.

"Awww, is that where she hid them? I never thought to look in her car!" Ray reached out and snatched one of the bars, immediately biting down on the wrapper at the end and ripping it open with his teeth.

"Oh my God, I bet your dentist loves you," I commented. The spectacle was a little like feeding time at the zoo. The hyena's cage, to be specific. "No thanks," I said when Ray offered me a bite. "Why's she hiding candy?"

"She and I have food issues." Ray wolfed down what was left of the Payday in a single chomp. Considering that he usually kept information about his personal life short and sweet, I thought that was the end of it. But no, he was only trying to get nougat out of his teeth. "Our family therapist says she expresses her frustration over my body choices by covertly trying to control my eating." The way Ray talked sounded as if he was quoting someone. Then, in his regular voice he added, "She thinks I'm fat. My dad bought these for me last August and they disappeared out of the grocery bags. Bitch."

Okay. Maybe there were advantages to not having a mom. I liked to pretend, when I was feeling low, that if my mom hadn't died she would fix everything wrong in my life, and that we'd have the perfect mother-daughter relationship and never raise our voices or argue about the stupid stuff my friends and their moms fought over. Yet I knew deep down inside that my stubbornness came straight out of her gene pool, and that if she were still alive, we'd probably be at each other's throats most of the time.

Of course, if the worst hadn't happened, we might still be in L.A. If she were around, I knew my dad wouldn't sit in front of the TV every night, tiring himself out so that when he finally went to bed he wouldn't have enough energy to cry himself to sleep. I knew our house wouldn't be the total pigsty it was now. I knew I'd be eating better.

But those things weren't what I wanted to think about, right then. We had a party to attend, and I was determined to have myself a good old time. Even if it killed me. I cleared my throat and averted my eyes from the spectacle of Ray wiping his mouth on the back of his sleeve. One thing I'll say about Ray: he surely had the mannerisms of a guy totally down. The only thing he seemed to be leaving out was letting go of occasional burps and grabbing his goodies . . . and yet I could live without the total authenticity. "So, Ray," I said, trying to sound jaunty yet casual, somewhere between girly-girl confidante and laid-back buddy. "If you were dating someone. . . ."

"I'm not dating anybody." He zoomed the Honda through a traffic light as it changed from red to green and turned onto a street lined by large, two- and three-story houses. Though it was getting darker by the minute, I could see the yellowed leaves of the trees overhanging the asphalt.

The smell of autumn always left me feeling a little melancholy. It's the scent of decay, isn't it, after all? I took another deep whiff. "Yeah, but if you were . . ."

"I'm not."

"Yeah, but if you were . . ."

"I'm . . ."

"If you say you're not, again, I'm going to throw the rest of those Paydays out the window," I threatened. That seemed to get his attention. "Okay. So *if* you were dating someone, which you're *not*, I know!" I added hastily, hearing his mouth open. "Would it be like . . ." Here's where I started to stumble. All week I'd tried to think of ways to ask Ray exactly what he might look for in a significant other. Specifically, the gender. I mean, I had no idea. Here I was, the person who'd last year pretended to cast curses on anyone who dared look at Ray cross-eyed, and I didn't have a clue who he was, or even who he wanted to date. Some kind of irony, huh? "Okay, introverted or extroverted?"

To my surprise, Ray didn't seem to mind answering that one. "Extroverted. But not like, totally flighty. Just outgoing. Like me."

"Outgoing like y—!" I bit back the rest of that sentence. Ray was the most introverted person I knew, but I was feeling generous. He could think of himself any way he liked. I could tell we'd reached the party. Dozens of cars lined the curb for two blocks. "Okay. Blond hair or brown hair?"

Ray pulled over to the side of the road and put the car into park. "Brown, I guess."

Nice. So far we were describing Tabitha to a T. Now for the tricky question. "Boy or girl?"

The engine died. "Marotti?"

Oh crud. Ray's voice was totally humorless. "Hmmm?"

The squeaky-clean act didn't fly with my teachers, and it certainly didn't fly with a friend who knew better. "What's going on?" I considered my options. I could keep playing innocent, and risk angering him, or I could tell him the truth. "Are you trying to hook me up?"

Naturally, I preferred the approach involving an outright lie. "No. Oh, no. God, no. Hook you up? Hah!" Though he'd stopped the car half a minute before, neither of us budged. Truthfully, I was afraid to move. "Maybe a little?" I finally admitted.

"V." Ray let both of his palms hit the steering wheel. "You told me . . . you said . . . I thought you wanted me to come because you wanted to hang out."

"Riiiight," I drawled, ladling on the mockery. "I told you, 'Ray, we haven't had a lot of hang-out time together. Let's go to the house of some guy who's rolling in dough on the night his kid's trashing the place, and enjoy some quality time.' " Right on cue, from inside the house three doors down, we heard a sudden blast of dance floor bass as one of the doors opened wide. A second later, it was muffled again, but still audible. " 'It'll be a nice, quiet evening, just you and me.' That's exactly what I said, hmmm?"

Ray knew the truth. I'd only had to say the words *party* and *Brandon Jerome* and he'd been pulling out the wad of index cards he kept in his back pocket as an organizer, so he could jot down the details. "I thought that since Gio wasn't coming, you were kind of asking me to, you know. Take his place." His voice sounded gruff and defensive.

"Gio's coming." It was my turn to sound oversensitive. Then again, how else was I supposed to behave when my boyfriend chose community service over me? "He's getting in a few more hours this evening so that the two of us can get in a whole day's worth of face time next Sunday. In fact, he should be here within the hour. Come on, let's go." I unbuckled my lap belt and climbed out of the car. "Come *on*," I repeated, once I'd slammed the door shut. For a second, through the window, Ray seemed as if he might actually drive away and leave me there. "It's not a hookup. You're the one who's been hinting I should introduce you around to these people. Ta-da! I'm your fairy godmother. Wish granted. Get your rear in gear, mister! We're going to be social if it kills us."

Massive is too mild a word to describe the relief I felt when Ray sighed deeply, slapped the steering wheel a final time, and popped open the driver's side door. "No love connections," he growled, straightening the lay of his bowling shirt, which sported his name embroidered in curly letters. Very retro. "And there better not be anybody lying in wait for me."

"No!" I said, with a guilty suspicion that Tabitha Hunter was probably wound up like a coil and ready to spring. "Oh, God no. Nothing like that!" He looked at me suspiciously as he stuffed his hands deep in the pockets of his jeans. "If you want, hang out with Addy and Brie. They're both probably already there. We can ignore everyone else and pretend we're the cool ones, for once."

Ray seemed to warm to that idea. He looked positively cheerful as we made our way past the other parked cars on the street in the direction of the Jeromes' house. Cheerful for Ray, that is. Anyone who didn't know him would have thought he was mourning a death in the family. Maybe of a puppy. He was probably writing a poem about me in his head, definitely on the unflattering side. "You know Brie wants to give our group a name," he said.

"Yeah, and I know that Brie's mom and dad named her after a hunk of cheese, and that didn't work out for the best, did it, now?" He snorted at that. Good. Maybe if I got him in a better mood now, he wouldn't blame me much once Tabitha cornered him.

No one answered the bell when I rang. Ray kind of rolled his eyes and pushed open the door. "It's not *that* kind of party," he said. How did everybody know better than me what kind of party this was? How come I was the only person who'd apparently never been to one of *those* kinds of parties?

Apparently it was because I treasured my eardrums. Listen, I'm no old lady. I like music. I like my music loud. But to be assaulted by N.E.R.D. at so high a volume that it felt like the vibrations might shake the flesh from my bones and reduce my skeleton to a pile of very fine ashes? Then to add to it the commotion of dozens of kids yelling at each other in order to be heard, and the sound of explosions from a group of guys playing Halo on the wide-screened TV at the living room's far end, and the shrieks and cackles of the girls watching them, as well as what sounded like the screeching of a dozen jammed blenders coming from the kitchen? That kind of made me feel like somebody's grandmother, wincing at the TV and complaining about the gosh-durned racket. Good gravy, but it gave me an instant migraine. "It's *loud*. Are my eyes bleeding?" I yelled at Ray.

He was too busy scanning the crowd to answer immediately. I saw his lips move and could barely make out his reply: "What?"

"Are my eyes . . . ?" He shook his head again. He still couldn't hear me. "Never mind!" I bellowed. "Let's go find Addy!"

"What?"

I was going to be hoarse before the night was over. I cupped my hands around my mouth and yelled right into his ear, "Let's! Go! Find! Addy!"

"No thanks!" Ray hollered back. "I already ate!"

Fan-freakin'-tastic. I jerked my head so he'd follow me through the crowd.

Okay, so maybe I hadn't been to many of these parties. I'm not the kind of person who needs to wear the hottest clothes or listen to the coolest music or hang out with the choicest people in order to feel good about myself. It wasn't my thing, you know? And man, if this is what all the parties were like, was I ever glad I'd never been invited. Nobody was doing anything horrible, exactly. It wasn't like one of those bad movies with Rich Kids Gone Wrong that ends with someone in the morgue, everyone else miserable, and the lead locked in a mental institution. Everywhere I looked, though, were high school kids trying to pretend they were college-aged. It was a little like some kind of costume party where everyone had come dressed up like big, swaggering adults, though they wore their usual clothes. Only their attitudes had changed. They'd grown bigger. The jocks who at school hung out on the bleachers buzzed on enormous bottles of Mountain Dew were crowded on the stairs here, watery-eyed from the cans of Budweiser they'd somehow managed to buy and drink. The girls who marched up and down the halls in their matching latest fashions, acting like the officers of some kind of occupying army, had taken over the entryways to each room, pretending to chat amongst themselves while really screening the people walking by. The ones who acted funny for attention, the ones who were the serious study-addicts, the ones who were desperate to get in good with the better crowds—they were all here, goofing for other people's laughter or holding beery intellectual conversations in the corners or stalking their superiors with a gleam of hunger in their eyes. The sight alone of all that alcohol made me distinctly uncomfortable. I began to wish I'd not come. The whole thing was all so phony. It made me a little sick.

I didn't know how superior I could feel, though. When I passed the guys on the stairs and a bunch of them shouted out at me with grins on their faces, and when I led Ray from the front hallway through the living room and into the dining room and the primped, pretty girls there waved and cocked their heads like they were surprised and glad to see me, I couldn't help but feel deep in my gut a little savage stab of satisfaction. *Finally*, it seemed to demand. *Finally, you know who I am!* So what did that say about me? That I was equally as phony?

I tried not to think about it. I had Addy and Brie to find. In the dining room, someone had bought a couple of party trays of nicely chopped up veggies and dip, but they were practically untouched, abandoned for the buckets of greasy chicken and the Doritos and the open boxes of pizza that lay mostly empty on the expensive glass dining table. Crumpled beer cans lay abandoned all around the edge of the table, like someone had set them up for target practice. I hadn't seen any older kids there; I didn't know who Brandon and his buddies had gotten to buy them so much beer. Maybe it belonged to his parents? I had no idea, and I didn't really care, since I didn't plan to be drinking any of that stuff. My dad would freak if he so much as smelled a whiff of it on my clothes.

We finally found Addy and Brie in the billiard room. The billiard room! The little house my dad and I rented didn't even have a separate area for a dining table. We had to eat our meals off little TV trays in the living room, or standing around the kitchen. The Jeromes had a whole room to hold a giant pool table with massive wooden legs carved as ornately as one of the Treasure Island ships in Las Vegas. Our friends sat on the edge of a crusty-looking leather sofa at the room's far end, legs crossed, facing each other as they eyed the boys playing pool. Some Goth chick sat on the sofa's arm right next to them. Over the back of the player bending down to take his shot, Addy saw us and waved. "Let's go over," I suggested to Ray at top volume.

"Huh? Who's a pet lover?" he yelled, his throat already scratchy from overuse. "Hey, let's go over!" *Yeah, Ray*, I wanted to say. *Brilliant idea, buddy*. I let it pass.

I could see why Addy and Brie had taken shelter with the ball-slingers, though; once we were out of the hall and through the doorway, the volume of all the music decreased by about half. Not until we were halfway across the room did I realize the Goth chick's identity, and then only when she sprang off the sofa and took a few quick steps in our direction. She reminded me of a deer in the forest when she suddenly stopped in her tracks and looked at us with dark, frightened eyes, uncertain whether we were friendly people bearing Bambi snacks, or big bad hunters with guns. I guessed it was up to me to make the introductions. "Ray, I think you know Tabitha? Tabitha Hunter?" Could he still not hear me? Had his eardrums ruptured? *"She was in your English class last year! Tabitha Hunter!"* I said loudly.

Too loudly, obviously. Ray gave me a pained look. "Dude. What's got in you tonight? Hey," he said to Tabitha. It was as offhand a *hey* as a girl could get without being brushed off entirely.

She dipped at the knee, waggled her fingers, and crinkled up her face in sheer delight. Considering her outfit, the coyness was a little bit distracting. She was wearing some kind of black leggings—a little bit like a pair I sometimes wore—the ends of which were stuffed into some leather-esque boots a lot like the ones I had on, in fact. And what had she done to her hair? What had happened to those perfect tresses finished off at the ends with a laser level? Now that I studied her closely, I was beginning to get an idea of where she'd gotten the evening's outfit. All that was missing was a rose quartz to match my pendant. "Nice T-shirt," I said, my voice composed. "I didn't know you were a Carbon Leaf fan."

"Oh my God," she enthused, grabbing my wrist. "Don't you just love them? I just love them. I didn't know you had a Carbon Leaf shirt!"

Oh yeah. She was cool as Arctic ice, that one. "Yeah, exactly like yours," I said. "In fact, I wore it Tuesday."

"I had *no* idea what to wear tonight so I came in what I had on. I probably look like a slob!" So was that what she thought of me while ripping off my personal style? *What would slobby ol' Vick wear?* "Do you get into Carbon Leaf?" she asked Ray. "They are *so* . . . "

"Move," Ray told her.

She responded with a blank, astonished face. "What?" So stricken did she look that I felt a little stab of guilt for my anger a moment before.

"Move." Ray repeated the word bluntly. When Tabitha didn't respond, he reached out and pushed her toward the wall. Every chivalrous bone in my body protested—guys shouldn't do that kind of thing. Especially Ray, the gentlest soul I knew!

But then one of the big beefalos playing pool said, "Thanks, guys," and bent over to complete his shot. The guy's cue extended right to the edge of where Tabitha had stood a moment before.

The relief she felt was plainly written all over her face. "Oh, I'm such a goof," she said, clucking, rolling her eyes, and giggling all at the same time. "For a minute there I thought you—"

After a sharp clack, the guy at the pool table straightened up and moved around to the other side. "Cool," Ray told Tabitha, scarcely seeming to notice her. "Talk to you later." He sauntered past, already greeting Addy and giving Brie a wave.

Ouch. Or as they say in Australia, crikey. Tabitha appeared stricken. What could I do but try to comfort her? I hated seeing people tramped on by others, even if out of carelessness, like I suspected it might have been with Ray. "It's kind of confusing in here isn't it?" I said, hoping she'd take the hint and buy it as an explanation. "So many people! Wow!"

I sounded lame. I knew it and she knew it. "I don't think he remembered me," she said, seeming to shrink. "I thought this would be more his type of . . . I'm an idiot." Oh, crud. I hated when people started to kick themselves. There are enough people in this world who are looking to beat you up—why help them out and do it to yourself?

"Well, I don't think he's a big Carbon Leaf fan." I took another look at her shirt. It was mine, all right. I mean, not *mine*. I hoped. If I got home and found she'd rifled through my T-shirt drawer, heads would roll.

"He doesn't like me. He doesn't, does he?" What in the world could I say? I could read Ukranian better than I could read Ray. "Is it the way I dressed? Come on, be honest. I can trust you."

The girl was putting me in a tight spot. I took a deep breath, leaned against the glossy red wall, and considered how to answer. "I don't think Ray's as concerned with the outside of people as with what's inside," I finally told her. The words had sounded okay in my head, but spoken aloud, they sounded right. "I mean, isn't that his whole thing? That the outside isn't what you really *are*? I mean, don't get me wrong," I said hastily. "He probably thought your outside was fine. But you know, you were kind of . . ."

Oops. I'd taken it too far. I clammed up before I could do any damage. Tabitha, though, had already caught on. "I did something, you mean? Oh God, it *was* all me, wasn't it?"

"No, no, not at all. I mean, you were a little bit . . ." I groped for a word.

"Needy?"

"Girly-girly," I said at the same time. Ugh. I hated being painted into a corner. This conversation could get so, so much worse, if she kept picking on herself. I didn't want to let her. "Listen," I said, trying to make amends. "Hang with us for a while. Be more like me. It'll be okay. Once he realizes you're into the same things, he'll open up. Ray's kind of . . . shy."

I could see her mulling over that one for a full half minute. Finally she nodded. Good. My life used to be so much easier when I didn't have to worry about anyone's hurt feelings except my own. "Yeah," she said, following me. "Shy. That's it." That was the sound of a girl trying to convince herself of something. I hoped it worked.

Addy gave me a quick and enthusiastic hug when I plopped down beside her on the sofa. The house was hot enough from so many people breathing and yakking that the leather was almost sticky to the touch. Brie leaned across Addy's lap to announce, "Red here thought you were going to wimp out." And I mean, she *leaned*. Both arms, as if she couldn't really support herself. "I told her she was wrong.

Wrong, wrong, wrong!" She made some emphatic arm movements, sloshing around the contents of her plastic cup.

Addy's smile of apology, sent my way, was for Brie. "What does it say about these parties when people come and hang with the same people they hang with at school?" she asked the group at large.

From her sprawled position in Addy's lap, Brie said with an arrogant flip of her blond hair, "It's a party. P-a-r-t-y. People hang out with who they want." Had she been drinking? I tried to take a sideways peek at what was in that red cup she held.

"But look at us." For someone who was trying to reason with a lump on her lap, Addy was surprisingly composed. Prim, even, as she held her own bubbling cola with both hands a distance above Brie's head. "What do we do in Chem? We all sit in the back together. Except you, Vick. Sorry."

"No problem," I said, not letting it show that it stung, being reminded I wasn't on the smart kids track.

"Then we all gravitate to the darkest and quietest corner of the cafeteria when we're not in class. There've got to be a good fifty or sixty people all over this house. We could be getting to know some of the kids we never talk to. But what do we do?" Addy threw up her hands. "We get together in the darkest and quietest room and huddle like . . ."

"Mummies," interjected Brie, unexpectedly.

". . . conspirators," Addy finished weakly.

Save for Tabitha, who from her perch on the sofa's arm had eyes only for Ray, the rest of us stared for a moment at the girl who wasn't exactly making the world's best case against dumb blonde jokes. "Mummies?" I asked at last. That was definitely beer she was drinking, I could tell now. I should have noticed the yeasty smell of it earlier, but with all the alcohol circulating around that party, tracking one scent of beer would have been like trying to find a grain of sugar in a teaspoon of sand. I reached for her cup. "This isn't doing you any good."

Right at the last second, she moved it out of reach and giggled. "It's not doing me any bad. Come on. Loosen up. It won't do you any bad, either."

This was one topic I really couldn't talk about rationally. Too many feelings were already coming to the surface, all of them angry. Addy noticed my raised eyebrows and appealing eyes and took the cue I desperately was trying to send her. "Come on, Brie. We didn't come here to get drunk."

"One beer. Not even a whole beer. I'm hardly drunk. Besides, if I wanted to get drunk, I could get what I wanted from my mom's liquor cabinet." She was right. I'd rarely seen Brie's mom without an iced drink in one hand and a cigarette in the other. Those were two of the reasons I didn't go over there very often.

"Give it a break already," Addy said. Then to me, she mouthed the word, "Sorry."

"Why?" Brie sprawled forward until her chin rested on my knee.

Ray had caught the entreaty in my eyes, too, because he leaned over and tried to pull Brie up. Tabitha, the silent Goth-ish angel hovering over his left shoulder, sat up, alert for a chance to help. "Brie, don't be a pain. You know why. Vick . . ."

"Vick's the pain. She's a pain because her boyfriend's not coming." Brie looked up, suddenly realizing whose leg her chin dug into. "Sorry. I've had a rough week."

"Tear," I said, pointing to my cheek, scorn turned to high.

"No, I'm really, really, really sorry!"

"Oh God. Drama!" I groaned. "Brie, sometimes you really know how to push my buttons." I yanked back my limbs and struggled to get to my feet.

"Aw, come on. I was just . . ."

I should have been watching more carefully. Right at the moment I jerked my knee, she rested her cup on it. An arc of beer flew into the air, glittering and gold. The liquid landed everywhere—the sofa, the oriental carpet, on all our feet—but mostly it somehow managed to fall in a cascade squarely onto my lap. Almost instantly I felt a lukewarm, fluid sensation as the stuff seeped through my jeans and began sticking to my skin. Even leaping up and dancing around couldn't prevent it from getting any worse. The stuff had already done its damage. "Holy cannoli!" I yelled at the top of my voice. "Brie, you stupid—!"

Of course, my timing was perfect. My yell coincided with the changing of the disc on the CD player. So when there was a relatively quiet moment where the only sound was of people talking normally without having to shout over the thumping, bumping bass— yeah, that was when I was doing my thing at the top of my lungs. I managed to pull out of my verbal nosedive right at the last second, totally aware that everyone in the room was staring at me. "Oh, shut up," I scowled at the pool players, who raised their eyebrows at each other. The music crashed down with another splat of guitars and drums, and they shrugged and went back to their game.

I had to give Brie some kind of credit. After the accident, she hadn't sat back and looked smug about it or anything, and she wasn't flouncing off, offended by the insult I'd nearly cast. In fact, both she and Addy immediately began using the Kleenex that Tabitha was pulling out of her pockets to sop up what they could. "Crap, I'm sorry," she said.

"Just . . ." I pushed Brie away. "I'm okay. Leave me alone." I didn't have expensive threads. Nothing was damaged. Except maybe my pride, a little.

Ray mopped up beer from the floor and ran his wad of tissues over sofa leather. Good thinking. I didn't want our little crew to be known as the kids who ruined Brandon Jerome's matching billiard room furniture. "I'm stupid. God, I don't know why you put up with me," Brie was saying while she dabbed at my shirt. "So *stupid*."

All the fuss bothered me. "Don't," I told her, trying to push her hands away.

"Come on, let me . . ."

"Don't!"

I really don't know whether it was my own hands trying to bat her away, or whether Brie snagged the chain herself. I felt a tug at the back of my neck, though, and saw a glint of gold as my pendant flew away. My fingers groped for the rose quartz that I'd barely removed from my neck since my birthday, but it was gone. "Now look what I've done!" Brie groaned. She dropped back to the floor. "Maybe it's under the sofa. I'm so, so sorry!"

I didn't need more drama. "It's a necklace, not a life-support system." The way Brie scolded herself as she scrabbled around looking for the gemstone made me uncomfortable. My soaked pants were making me uncomfortable. Losing the pendant made me uncomfortable. Hell. The entire party and everyone at it made my skin so itchy that I wanted to run away and put as much space between me and everybody else as possible. I shouldn't have come. Why had I? To help out Ray? To help out Tabitha?

Or had I come—and the thought made me itchier still—solely for the purpose of showing Gio that I could fit in at one of his friends' events? I shouldn't have been there at all. "I smell." When I said the words, I was aware of how freaky I must have looked. My face was screwed up in a scowl. You know how parents are always complaining about us elevating their blood pressure? Well, my face was so hot and puffy that I knew right then exactly what they meant. The room was suddenly too hot to stand. I began to feel dizzy. I had to get my jeans off. I had to get them *off right then*. Panic had set in—I really, really had to change. I smelled. I was covered with alcohol. Where was Gio? Why wasn't he there? I needed to get out of that room. I needed to get out of those pants. "Addy?" I said, so weakly that I knew she couldn't hear.

Yet she looked up anyway, at first to see if there

were any other spots she could try to blot. "Vick?" I saw her mouth. She stood up, and held me by the elbow. "It's okay. Let's get you to a bathroom. Hold on one sec," she murmured in my ear, before turning to tell the others something.

I'm a pretty tough girl. Pride myself on it. I'd always thought of myself as a kind of fortress—strong, protective, invincible. But you know, fortresses could fall. I half-remembered a Sunday school story about a city that crumbled to dust from a blast of trumpets. Funny, how in one stupid moment all my defenses came tumbling down. That city was me. All it took was a stupid dousing in beer to do it. The other kids couldn't see, though. I wouldn't let them watch me cry. My pendant was gone. Where was Gio? He would have understood. Internally, I begged Addy to hurry.

"Let me come," I heard Brie say, in response to whatever Addy had told them. "It's my fault."

Nuh-uh, I thought to myself, right at the same time Addy shook her head and murmured a quick something in Brie's ear. What had she said? *Good going, Brie. That dead mom Vick never talks about? Killed by a drunk driver. And you had to go cover her in beer.* No, Addy would have been nicer than that. I don't think she had it in her to make anyone else feel badly over a stupid mistake. Her hand was on my arm now; I could smell the sweet, vanilla-y scent of her shampoo over my own foul odor. "Come on," she urged, guiding me past the pool table and toward the door. "We'll get you cleaned up."

"Gio can take me home," I told her. Every step I

took was sheer torture; the wet denim clung to my skin when I moved. I really didn't want to be there anymore. "He should be here by now. Can you find him? Find him and tell him to take me home?"

"He's not here," she said, not meeting my eyes. "Come on, we'll find someplace private."

"Wait. What do you mean, he's not here?" I asked her. I didn't care how miserable I looked, with my hair hanging down around my face and my black clothes made even darker by their soaking. I could tell when Addy was hiding something from me. She wasn't a good liar at all. "Tell me."

She rubbed at her forehead. A year ago, when we'd first become friends, Addy's cheekbones had been covered with freckles. When had they started to fade? Her skin still reddened at the slightest hint of embarrassment, though. "Don't get upset," she said in the vicinity of my ear, stalling. Oh, I'd already stopped in for a visit to Upset, then abandoned it for Dismayed, and had hopped on the next bullet train headed for Freakin' Perturbed. "Gio sent a text message before you and Ray got here. I was going to tell you," she protested, when my mouth opened wide. She fished in her pocket while she talked. "But I didn't want to do it in front of everyone. Brie saw it, though."

She was only adding to my panic. "Is something wrong? Is he okay?" My fingers scrabbled for her cell phone as she held it out in my direction. I flipped open the little pink clamshell and let her push a couple of buttons for me. On the screen, beneath Gio's name and cell number, was a series of blocky letters that spelled out the message: TELL LADY V. I'M VOLUNTEER-ING AN EXTRA THREE HOURS & WILL SEE HER TOMORROW. IT'S ALL GOOD. GIO.

I couldn't believe my eyes. I'd come to this lousy party for *him*, and he wasn't going to be there? I barely was aware of handing back the phone. There was no point in throwing it across the room when it wasn't mine. "You know what?" I told Addy. "Boys suck."

She shrugged. "Yeah. Pretty much. But—"

"But me no buts," I shouted over my shoulder. Moments before I'd felt weak and defenseless. Now, though? I felt my control coming back, thanks to the sweet, familiar feeling of anger. I didn't give a flying flip what the Oostermonster said. Anger could be my friend. "Suck is the word." I turned and nearly careened into a wall of jock muscle.

"Word for what?" Brandon Jerome, fabled over-privileged senior and resident of a house with its own billiard room, leaned carelessly against the door frame. Had he been born with that sneer, or had it swelled along with his dad's savings account? Ugh. Why had I thought that any party of his might be interesting? Behind him was a squadron of his comrades—Tyler Woodwell, Artie Costello, Michael Brice. "What's wrong, Marotti, don't you think *suck* can be a pretty nice word? Maybe I should ask your boyfriend, Carson."

"Funny," I told him, crossing my arms and playing it cool. "Maybe I should ask *yours*. Whatcha think, Tyler?"

Was that a twitch of a smile I saw on Tyler's face? It

was no fun if they didn't get upset. Brandon didn't even flinch. "Pee yourself, Marotti?"

I followed his nod, and looked down at myself. Oh, crispy critters. It *did* look like I'd had some kind of uncontrollable preschool accident. Was that why everyone was staring at me? I glanced around. The guys playing pool were snickering in my direction, saying something behind their hands. Artie and Michael were rubbing their mouths, as if about to laugh. The observation threw me enough off-balance that for a few seconds I could only gape.

Thank God for Addy, who snapped out, "She spilled, moron."

"Spilled her bladder?" Yeah, because you see, when you have all the advantages of wealth and privilege, it's best to utilize them for quality urine jokes.

"Don't be an ass, Brandon." Tyler shoved his friend out of the way. "Come on," he said to me, taking me by the arm more gently than I would have guessed he might. "I'll get you guys to a bathroom."

I found myself being tugged through the hallway, which was much more crowded than when we'd arrived. "Get the girl some Depends while you're at it, Woodwell!" I heard Brandon call after me.

"Charming host," Addy snarled, curling her lip in disgust. "Really charming!" she yelled back. Good old Addy.

Tyler continued pulling me through the throng. His only reply was to raise his free hand and, in the direction of Brandon, let loose with a nice, ripe, perfect flip of the middle finger.

On the whole, I liked his response better.

CHAPTER SIX

"Vick, you've *got* to get in here." Surrounded by so much marble, Addy's voice echoed with the special effects reverb of a movie monster speaking from the tomb. Well, a really nice, young movie monster. With long, straight red hair and a practical pair of jeans and a sweater vest. And instead of tentacles, legs propped up on the bathtub wall, right above its gold faucet. "You could drown a person in here. You could swim!"

Being in little more than my bra and panties makes me a little untalkative. "That's nice," I said, making a mental list of people to drown.

"When I get a good job, I want a bathtub like this," she sighed happily. "Big. Marble. On a pedestal. With bubbles."

"Mmmm." I was too furious to have a real conversation. Not furious with Addy—with Gio. Ditching me at the last minute, and telling me through a text message! Not even to my own phone! Okay, so I couldn't afford my own cell phone, but still!

102

"I bet these are the Jacuzzi jets, right here." While I rinsed the washcloth I'd been using to wipe off my sticky thighs, she suddenly sat up and began studying the hardware. "There's a digital temperature control for the shower. And *two* nozzles." When she stood up, the flats of her shoes hit the tub's inside with a slap. "I wonder why the second nozzle?" she asked, reaching out for the one pointed roughly at her midsection. Then, thinking about it, she giggled, "Oh!"

"Do you think he's seeing someone?" I couldn't help my question. It flew out loaded with poison, like a curare-laced arrow. "Because if he is . . ."

"Who? No!" Addy tore herself from the bath and tile aisle at last, sat on the tub's edge, and watched me. "I don't think he's seeing anyone. Wait, you mean Tyler, right?"

"*Tyler?* Why would I mean Tyler?" I screeched, amazed.

"He's the one who led us up here. I thought . . ."

"No! I mean Gio!"

"Oh. Gio."

It's frustrating when your best friend isn't following your train of thought. It's doubly frustrating when she thinks you're talking about some loser you barely know. Add to that the bland way she'd said those last two words, and anybody would understand why I wanted to run screaming out of the house, fast as the cartoon Road Runner, leaving behind only clean Vick-shaped outlines in any walls or doors that got in my way. "You think Gio's seeing someone?!" I yelled.

"Ssssh," she warned. "You sound like a crazy lunatic girl."

"I am a crazy lunatic girl!" All around town, there were probably dogs whining and covering their floppy ears with their paws from the shrill sound of my voice. I took it down a notch. "Oh, crud. He *is* seeing someone else."

"Why would you think that?" Addy, my personal voice of reason, shook her head. "He has you."

I appreciated that she looked so puzzled about it. "Because . . ."

Sometimes if you don't talk about a thing, it feels like it's not real. If you don't put it into words, it can't hurt you. I should have known how stupid that was in this case, because fear had been gnawing at me from the inside for a week now without me saying a single syllable. How much worse could it be if I were to unload a little? "Vick, what?" Addy prompted.

I cleared my throat. I'd made a decision. "It's like this," I said slowly. At first I had to force out the words, as I told her about how I'd thought I'd seen Gio and some other chick at the mall, when he'd allegedly been volunteering. By the time I got to the part where he'd admitted not telling me about this stupid, loud, obnoxious party, I was babbling. "Maybe I'm not good enough for him. No, I know I'm not. I'm totally wrong for him, right? He's better off with someone more like him. Someone like—"

A shrill set of squeals from a coven of girls roaming the upstairs hallway interrupted us, followed by a knock. "Can we come in?" some girl called through the door, jiggling the knob.

"It's occupied," I called out.

"What?"

Addy got right up, marched over to the door, opened it, poked out her head, and said, "*Ocupado*."

"But . . ."

"Scram," she announced, then shut the door firmly and re-locked it again. I loved Addy right then. I was scratching at my no doubt puffy eyes when she returned across the fluffy carpet to her tubside perch. "Vick," she said, arms crossed. "You're being a big drama queen."

"I am not!" I said, realizing too late that stomping my foot at the same time probably wasn't helping defend my case. "Tonight was supposed to be all about the two of us doing one of *his* things instead of sitting around his living room watching DVDs or playing video games or practicing for some kid's birthday party magic show or . . ."

"How do you know those aren't his things?" Addy pointed out. "A boy wants to get all cuddlesome at home with you and you're *complaining* about it?"

I glared at her as I fiddled with my top. It was as dry as it was going to get, after being sponged at and laid out to parch under the bathroom's overhead heat lamp. "Gio's a boy. And popular. This is the kind of thing he used to do before me," I explained, pulling it on. The dampish section hit me squarely in the belly.

"Have a little trust. He could still do it if he wanted."

"Exactly. With some other girl," I said, surprised at my anger. "You're proving my point!"

Addy pulled her lips to one side. I always thought of that expression as her schoolmarm scowl. "Okay. Look. All I'm saying is that if Gio didn't want to stay in, he wouldn't. Right?" Wrong. Gio was such a nice guy that if his girlfriend was too dirt-poor to do anything but hang at home nights with him, he'd do it, even if she never once admitted that money was the reason. But Addy didn't need to know that about me. "Why would he say he was at the senior center if he wasn't?"

"Some girl," I said darkly.

"*Or*," Addy said with emphasis, "maybe he's getting in some more volunteer hours at the center, like he said. Hmm. What's the simplest answer?"

"Simple, shmimple."

"It's called Occam's Razor."

"Occam, shmocc . . ."

"Vick." Again with the schoolmarm scowl. "Everything boils down to one issue. Do you trust Gio?" Great, ask me the one question I didn't want to answer. I shook out my jeans, stepped into the legs, and started to pull them up my perfectly ordinary non A-list thighs and hips. I'd bet anything that the girls there that night all had perfect, *O.C.*-quality thighs without an ounce of cellulite, and that any of them would be mad to have Gio for their own. They couldn't pinch more than an inch, no sirree. I was Hamburger Helper in a filet mignon world. Gio knew that at heart. And yet, he'd stuck by me for months and months now. Why? Addy wouldn't let go of her question. Like a dog with a juicy T-bone, she was. "Well, do you?"

When finally I'd buttoned up my jeans and smoothed my hands over the still-damp sections, I said, "You know Brie's going to be all oh-my-God-did-you-know-Vick's-mom-was-killed-by-a-drunk-driver-so-now-she's-a-psycho-whenever-she-sees-someone-with-a-drink all over school on Monday, don't you? If she hasn't already. What?" I asked, letting my eyes flick over to Addy. Still with the scowl! Didn't those muscles ever get tired? "I'm not a psycho about that, you know. I just had beer all over me, and . . ."

"Avoidance, much?" Her accusation brought my mouth to a halt. "Do you?" I grimaced. She was actually going to make me say it, wasn't she? "Do you trust . . . ?"

"I know the question." My words came out snappish. "Are you going to lecture me?"

"Maybe." She stared at me a moment, then began to fish into her pocket again. "Okay," she said at last, holding out her cell phone. "If you don't trust him, call him."

Tempting. It was very, very tempting. "Oh, right," I said, still staring at the little pink phone only inches from my nose. "What's he going to say if he answers from, I don't know, the back row of some drive-in movie where he's making out with some slut and I ask where he is? *Oh sure, I'm still at the senior center, can't you hear the bingo in the background?*"

"There are no drive-in movies in this county," Addy said. "And I didn't mean call his cell phone. If you don't trust him, call the center and ask to speak to him." I had to hand it to Addy. She came up with plans nearly as cunning as my own. For a moment I stared at the phone, shiny and beckoning, knowing pretty much what Eve had felt like in Eden when the nice serpent offered her a honkin' big slice of apple strudel.

After what felt like an eternity, I shook my head. "Nah," I told her, remaining firm when she waggled the phone. "Forget it. I'm probably being a drama queen, like you said." At last she removed temptation from my face. "I guess that spill freaked me out a little more than I wanted to admit," I said, turning to the enormous mirror over the glass washbasins. "Stupid."

Touching up in the mirror is the universal girly-girl sign for *let's get ready to rejoin the world*, you know. Once I started, Addy scooted over, lickety-split, to examine her porcelain-white skin and the fall of her hair. Weird to think it was so stylish and straight now, when it had been a frizzy nightmare last spring. People change, right? Wasn't that what this was all about? "You're not stupid," she assured me. "You're letting worry get you carried away."

"Yeah." I was done. "You're right. I'm being a little over-the-top. That's all." She finished up and turned to me, obviously pleased I'd come round to her way of thinking. The satisfaction on her face made me a little sad, actually, but I pretended to be relieved. "Why don't you head downstairs?" I suggested, keeping my words casual. "I'll be right there."

"I can wait," she said.

"I kind of need a couple of minutes to myself. It'll be okay." When we walked to the door, Addy took one last regretful look around the immense bathroom. I put a hand on her shoulder. "Thanks for being here for me."

Addy's eyes grew round. "That's what I'm here for!"

I let her squeeze my hands. At last she slipped out and was gone. I latched the door and leaned against it, exhaling. That had been one little show I'd put on, there. Oh, I was really happy that Addy was my friend, but all the other stuff where I'd pretended that the idea of checking up on Gio didn't appeal to me? I totally deserved some kind of Academy Award.

Oh, sure, I was all kinds of dishonest. But wasn't it kinder, really, to Addy and to everybody else if I didn't bug them with my doubts? I'd pretend everything was peachy keen for their sakes. Even if it killed me. They didn't need to know about my Gio worries any more than they needed to know about my home woes. Across the cavernous room—who really needed a bathroom bigger than my dad's living room, anyway?—I looked at myself in the mirror. Slouched. Scowling. Mean. That was the Vick I knew. That was the Vick who was going to leave the room, push her way through the crowd, and disappear home.

My plans were squashed the instant I opened the door. Some giggly girl and one of the track team guys immediately slithered past, probably intent on some kind of bathroom make-out session. "Sorry, Vick," said the girl as she knocked against me in passing.

The fact she knew my name when I didn't have a clue about hers cheesed me off, for some reason. "Try the tub," I barked at the closed and latched door. "I hear it's positively spacious. Losers," I growled.

"'Sup?" I heard a voice say behind me. When I turned, Tyler Woodwell stood there, arms crossed, leaning against the hallway wall, wool cap pulled low. "Feel better?"

"Do you wear that hat everywhere?" I asked him. "I mean, indoors and out? School and home? Church? Summer, winter, spring, fall? Everywhere? What does it mean, the ubiquitous wool cap? Is its very shabby ordinariness what makes it so worthy of envy, so desirable? Is its coolness inverse in proportion to its actual attractiveness? Or is it simply to cover up that you didn't shampoo today? Explain," I said, looking up into the stratosphere where his height seemed to end. "On second thought, never mind."

When I tried to push by, he restrained me with a hand on my shoulder. We both turned our heads in the direction of the main staircase when, from down below, came the sound of glass breaking on the floor. Animals! "What I don't get," he said, looking back at me once again, "is how a girl who uses words like *ubiquitous* manages to end up in so many Sped classes."

"So many what?" I asked, voice dangerous.

"Aren't you in Sped math and science? Sped," he repeated. "Special edu—"

"Don't," I warned him, holding up a hand. "And I'm not. Vice Principal Oostergard put me *temporarily* in what she calls 'sections for the life-stressed.' "

"Yeah. Sped," he repeated.

"I can't believe I'm talking to you," I growled, annoyed beyond endurance. Why was he needling me? My exasperation at Tyler never for a minute made me forget the other irritation at hand, though, so instead of heading downstairs where it sounded like three or more guys had begun some kind of bellowing match at the tops of their lungs, I hesitated and asked, "Do you have a cell phone?"

"Yeah, sure," he said, puzzled, as if I'd asked him the periodic number of magnesium. "You want . . . ?"

When he began digging through his back pocket for it, I held out a hand. The noise from below was getting worse; it sounded almost like some kind of brawl had broken out. "Can we go outside or something?" I yelled over the commotion.

"Yeah. Sure. Follow me."

Tyler must have visited Brandon's home many times before, because he knew it like the back of his hand. Not that he could have read the back of his hand, since it had grabbed mine so he could pull me down toward the darker end of the carpeted upstairs hall-way. For a second I almost protested, but sure enough, there was some kind of narrow back stair-well I'd not noticed before that led downstairs. It was strangely deserted. When we at last spilled out into a breakfast room off of the kitchen, I saw why—just about everyone was crowding in the direction of the living room, where all that arguing was still going on. With the music at top, insane volume, several guys were yelling at the tops of their lungs. There was a sound of someone hitting the wall, probably with all his weight, followed by more yelling.

Tyler pulled me in the opposite direction and to-ward a pair of French doors at the back of the break-fast room right as another crash of glass cut through the ruckus. "Ouch," he winced. "Lucy's gonna have some 'splainin' to do!"

After the hothouse humidity of the party, the cold October night air instantly chilled every moist part of my body, freezing me as thoroughly as a sub-zero cooler. On the whole, I liked it much better. A couple of kids who had been smoking on the deck stubbed out their cigarettes and stood up. "What's going on in there?" one of them asked.

"Testosterone run amok?" I suggested.

"Someone's fighting," Tyler explained. That was all they needed to get them to their feet and inside. Once the door closed, we were alone. Though from within I could still hear the *thump-thump-thump* of the music and the roar of male voices, out here it was relatively quiet. My eardrums throbbed from the contrast. "So do you—?" Tyler started to ask, reaching again for his phone.

In the house next door, a light went on and one of the upstairs windows suddenly shot up with a *whoosh*. "You damned kids are too damned loud!" shouted a middle-aged woman in curlers. We could really only see the outline of her head and shoulders, with the light behind her, but she sounded pretty mad.

"It's not our party, ma'am," Tyler called out. I was a little surprised at how polite he could be.

"I don't care! You kids have gone too far this time! I've called the police!" she yelled, pulling herself indoors. With another *whoosh*, the window slammed shut.

In the dim yellow light spilling onto the deck from the house, Tyler and I looked at each other for a quick second, then broke out into subdued laughter. "Crazy," I said, shaking my head and sitting down.

"I'm not sure I'd want to live next to the Jeromes tonight, either." Tyler turned something over in his hands as he sat next to me. Not too close, I noticed.

"I thought Brandon was one of your buds."

"There are buds, and there are buds." I could appreciate that sentiment. I really could. "So," he said, holding out a battered cell phone. Judging from its heft, it wasn't this year's latest model. "You want?"

I took it in my hands with a nod. "Thanks," I said, turning it around. The plastic was still warm. Although it was cold and breezy, I felt more alert out here than I had in the house.

We sat in silence for a long, long time before he spoke again. "Need me to show you how to use it?"

"I can manage, thanks." The big question, of course, was whether I wanted to. Addy had been right. It all came down to trust. If I called the senior citizen center, wouldn't I be betraying everything? This whole situation felt like stepping onto an expanse of frozen lake, knowing that one wrong, irrevocable step would send cracks running in crazy vectors along the ice. Those were the kind of cracks that could never again be repaired.

We'd sat there in quiet for a while when he spoke again. "You know, that day you beat me up at school . . ."

"I didn't!" I protested, then thought back. Did he

mean when he'd broken his leg? Or last week? "Which one?"

"See? You have to ask!" Over my chagrin, he kept talking, sounding more pleased than upset or anything. "Monday. Remember? Anyway, I was going to tell you something."

I couldn't let go, though. "You know, technically, I didn't beat you up either time. The only thing I did Monday was to grab your collar and shake you around a little." He whuffed out air that I could read as plainly as words: *like that wasn't enough to land you in the Oostermonster's office?* "And I wasn't even around when you broke your leg last year."

"Yeah, I know," he said, to my surprise. "Nobody much was around when I broke my leg. After, I mean." He turned his head to look at me. "One of the weird things about sports is that you're only as good as your last game."

"Please." I put my best *let's get real here* tone to use. "You jocks get all the attention from everybody. Homecoming in this town gets more hype than the Superbowl does anywhere else. What do you want me to say, *poor little jock boy* while I play my teeny-tiny violin? Tear."

He ignored the way I pointed to my cheek. "When I was sidelined, I was really sidelined," he said, stuffing his hands in his jeans pockets. "I don't mean that I didn't get to play ball like I did before. I was totally, completely, utterly out of the loop, going to physical therapy instead of hanging out after school, staying home with my leg up instead of doing the parties and the pep rallies and all that crap." He must've caught my chuckle, because he said, "Yeah, it's crap, I know. One of the things you find out real quickly when you have a fall from grace is how everyone else thinks about the stuff you always took for granted. Like pep rallies? Everybody who doesn't attend—which is like, everybody—thinks they're crap. Football games? Crap. Homecoming? Crap. School spirit?"

"Let me guess. Crap?"

"Pretty much. You know what's worse?" I shook my head. Although I still wasn't completely buying his sob story, at least for now I was listening. "Being on crutches and watching all the people you thought were your friends run off ahead of you, and realizing that they were full of crap, too."

"It's a regular crap-fest."

"It's like you're not a real person anymore. Just some kind of character named *Poor Tyler*. Only the pity doesn't last long, and after a while you become totally invisible." I'd been invisible enough times in my life that I could sympathize with that one. "But what really bites is when you're visible enough that you start to hear what other people are saying about you."

"I can't believe your jock buddies would badmouth you to your face," I told him.

"Not the jocks. They're a tiny, tiny little . . . hey, did you see *Titanic*?" I cocked my head and gave him a hostile look. I was so not playing King of the World with Tyler Woodwell. "Okay, so you know that when you see an iceberg floating in the ocean, the part above water is only like, ten percent of the whole iceberg. There's this massive block of ice underneath it, supporting it, ready to rip the *Titanic*'s hull into shreds." Here he ran through a gamut of sound effects lifted directly from the movie, from the grinding of ice against metal to the splash of incoming water to the deep bass groan of the ship breaking apart. If I hadn't been in so stern a mood, I might've laughed. "Anyway, one of the things I found out is that school's a lot like that iceberg. There's this little itty-bitty frozen bit that everyone sees—all the jocks and the academic superstars and the leads in the spring musical and the kids you know are going to end up on the FBI Most Wanted list and the prettiest most popular girls, all of them—and then there's a huge, anonymous mass that no one knows about."

I had to disagree with him on that one. "You mean, there's a huge anonymous mass that none of you guys in the top ten percent bother to notice."

"What're you talking about?"

"I'm saying, that none of you guys . . ."

He stopped me. "No, I mean, why do you say *you guys?*"

For a second, I was speechless. The fight inside the house was apparently still going on, because I could hear a number of people yelling out in dismay after what sounded like heavy furniture turning over. I let the uproar fill the silence. "What are you implying?" I asked at last, careful to let him know he was treading on dangerous territory.

"Come on, Marotti. Do you really think people don't know who you are?" When I opened my mouth to protest, he cut me off. "Seriously. You've gone out of your *way* to make sure *everybody* knows who Vick the Great and Terrible and her friends are."

His words filled me with a cold fury. "Oh, please! Okay, so some people might know my name, but there isn't a single person in the school who wants to be like me. I'm not one of the prettiest girls, or an academic superstar . . ."

"I don't see you trying out for the spring musical either," he said, confidentially. "Maybe the Most Wanted list is more your speed."

"Hah. Funny. Only, you know, kind of not." I jabbed his phone's antenna against my knee. "What do you want from me, Woodwell? You want me to pretend I'm popular so that you'll feel better about all the awful things you ever said about me?"

"I never said anything bad about you!" he protested. "When you laid that curse down that everyone said broke my leg, it was Barry Ota you got into a smack-down with. I was there when you went all freaky one afternoon and those words started appearing on your arms out of nowhere, and that's why later on people were all, 'Oh wow, Vick cursed Poor Tyler.' But I was in the background!"

"Whatever." People who had to be one hundred percent accurate annoyed me when I wanted to play fast and loose with the facts.

"There's nothing . . ." His words trailed off. "What's that noise?"

I didn't hear anything at first, but when I listened hard, I could hear the keening of sirens in the distance. "I guess that lady really did call the cops. Huh."

"I'm glad we're out here and not in there," he said.

Though I was shivering a little, I nodded. "No kidding."

"Anyway, there's nothing I want from you. Well, maybe you could treat me a little nicer, what with me lending you my phone and all." I couldn't help but roll my eyes. At the same time, though, I knew he was right. Apparently I owed him for a broken leg, too. "All I'm saying is that when I went down into the underwater part of the iceberg, I got to hear everything people were saying about the upper ten percent. It was an eye-opener."

"If you're trying to tease me into asking what people say about me, I don't care." I was lying. Of course I was wildly interested. Who wouldn't be? Yet some things are better left unheard, and there was no way I'd ever, ever beg him to repeat any of it.

"You're spiky," he commented.

"Just noticing that, are you?" I snapped. "And you're nosy."

"Okay, Nosy Guy has something else to say, then. You know that free lunch card you were trying so hard to hide from me the other day?" Oh, he knew he had me when he heard my sharp intake of breath. "Yeah, the one you seem to treat like a badge of shame. Carried one myself for three years, thanks, when my folks were both unemployed."

He had to go there, did he? Maybe I did have anger management problems. Right at that moment, I surely wasn't managing so well, and anybody could hear it in my voice. "So, what, the fact that we both get at least one free meal a day suddenly makes you an expert on me?" Never, ever, ever would I admit that sometimes lunch was the only hot meal I got.

"Hey, calm down."

I leapt to my feet. "Don't . . . !" I couldn't tell whether my mood was affected by the sirens, or vice versa. Judging by their volume, they seemed to have parked outside the front of the house. I could see splotches of red light cross the side of the neighboring house from time to time. "I'm fine," I barked. "I'm calm! I'm not un-calm! I don't need . . . !"

What a lame way to finish a sentence. "What don't you need?" he asked quietly, when I couldn't continue. "What *do* you need?"

Though flashers lit up the brick walls of the adjoining house and streaked across the leaf-strewn grass in a hypnotic rhythm, the sirens had gone silent a few seconds before. "To make a phone call," I said with sudden decision, punching out the numbers 4-1-1.

"Directory assistance, city, state, and the party you wish to reach, please," I heard a bored adult say. I gave her the information. "Please wait while I connect you to your party."

Tyler was making a show of pretending not to listen, but there was no way he couldn't overhear. For some reason, I didn't really care. If he wanted to be one of the faceless submerged majority, fine. Let him be. I had a vision of that girl I'd bumped into upstairs, and how she'd known my name when I didn't have a clue about hers. Talk about guilt. I flushed all over with the stuff, right as someone put an end to the bleeps I'd been hearing. "Sycamore Point Senior Citizen's Center," I heard a woman say. "Our visiting hours are over for the day. May I help you?"

Oh, God. I'd taken that step onto the ice. I could feel it cracking beneath my toes. Panic made me suddenly sweaty again, despite the cold. "Um," I said, somewhat inanely.

"Hello?"

Pull yourself together, girl, I told myself. *It's just a phone call.* "I was wondering if Gio Carson was still working," I said, keeping my voice low, especially when I pronounced Gio's name. Would Tyler figure out what I was doing? "He's a student volunteer."

"Who?" she said, instantly confirming all my worst fears. She'd had no clue who he was. I was going to die alone and miserable because my boyfriend was cheating on me. Then she exclaimed, "Oh! Gio!"

"Yes!" I said, sounding as grateful as a puppy given a Milk-Bone. "Gio Carson. Is he still there? I don't want to talk to him or anything," I said, hurriedly. "I was . . ."

"Who is this?" the woman asked with suspicion. I could picture her in my mind, kind of roly-poly and regal, like the millionaire's wife on *Gilligan's Island*. Maybe she could hear the booming music in the background. As if by magic, it suddenly shut off.

"This is . . . his . . ." I peeked over at Tyler. He was regarding me frankly, now. ". . . mother," I improvised, clearing my throat.

"Ohhhhhhh!" I almost had to hold the phone away from my head. "You must be so proud of your little Gio! Everyone here loves him. Such a sweetheart."

"He is?" I asked, then quickly amended, "I mean, I know. I get that all the time."

"I can imagine! So energetic and cheerful and always has a good word for everyone. That's our Gio. I know I saw him a little earlier, but let me see if I can . . ."

"No," I babbled. "That's okay. I don't need . . ."

"Oh, it won't take me a moment. Please hold."

The heck I would. I jabbed at the end-call button and nearly dropped the phone in my hurry. I mean, yikes. What was Gio going to think when the receptionist told him his mom had called? Well, that would hardly be unusual. But what if he checked the caller ID and saw it had been me? Oh, wait. This wasn't my phone. I wiped it on my jeans and handed it back to Tyler. "Tell anyone about this and you'll be back in physical therapy," I warned.

He raised his eyebrows. "Checkin' up on the boyfriend, huh? Never a good sign."

"Shut it!" I said, pointing at him. I rose to my feet with what little dignity I still had. Inside, I was trembling. I shouldn't have made that call.

"You got it, Marotti," he joked. "Or should I call you Mrs. Carson?"

I pointed again and walked in the direction of the breakfast room door. Now that it was quieter, maybe I could go back and find my pendant. "Shut!"

He tagged along behind. "You're pretty foxy for a soccer mom, Mrs. Carson!"

"It!"

I zipped my fingers together right as the back door opened and two police officers stepped out. One of them immediately blinded me with a flashlight beam in my corneas, making me reel. I stumbled a little, only catching myself from falling at the last moment. "We've got two more out back," said one of the men into a com unit on his shoulder.

Meanwhile, the closer of the two had taken a good

whiff of me and drawn his own conclusions. "How old are you?" he asked.

"Why?" I wasn't trying to be defiant. I wanted to know.

"She reeks of beer," he said to his buddy.

Tyler spoke up then, God bless him. "She hasn't been drinking, officer. I've been with her the entire time."

"Mmm-hmmm. And I'm Porky Pig, son. You're both coming along with us."

We both protested, but it was no use. Because, you know. It's not really good enough that I had to endure a hundred social humiliations at my first big party. It totally made sense that I had to get myself arrested at its end, too.

CHAPTER SEVEN

". . . And it seems to me, given your recent outbursts, up to and including your arrest . . ."

"I wasn't arrested." Well, I hadn't been! I wouldn't pretend otherwise, not for the sake of the Ooster-monster and her precious clipboard.

"Vickie . . ."

"It's Vick, okay? And I wasn't! There were no charges, okay? I wasn't behind bars. I didn't wear a little striped uniform!"

Mrs. Oostergard looked up at that, and peered at me over the top of her reading glasses. "Striped uniform?"

That dame really picked up on the oddest things. She didn't listen to one word about what was really happening right beneath her snotty little nose, but bring up something weird and she was all ears. "Like the prisoner on the Monopoly 'Get Out Of Jail Free' card. Honestly, Ms. Oostermon—I mean, Oostergard, all I did was sit on the chairs until my dad came to get me."

Now we were back on track. She withdrew an orange sheet of paper and studied it. "Which he neglected to do until shortly after midnight . . ."

"Fifteen minutes after they let me call. I'd say that was pretty speedy!"

"Apparently, he told Officer . . . Burke . . . that he was unaware of his daughter's drinking problem."

Oh, good gravy. We were so not going there. "I don't drink," I told the woman. "They gave me a breathalyzer. Which I passed, thank you."

Here came that false smile again. She could turn it on and off at will, but mostly it came on whenever she was about to gloss over the truth and head straight to Fantasyland. "Vickie."

"Vick."

"In light of recent events, Mr. O'Doul and I think . . ." To tell the truth, I'd forgotten Counselor O'Dull was in the room with us. He hadn't said a word. Was he sleeping? It was impossible to tell, his glasses and beard were so thick. "We agree that without adequate parental guidance, it may be advisable . . ." My brain must have been caught in some kind of slo-mo special effects filter. The vice principal's words kept flowing, but I seemed to comprehend only about one in ten. ". . . seems obvious . . . *in loco parentis* . . . asleep at the wheel, as it were . . ." My breathing sounded unnaturally loud. Something bad was coming. I was sure of it. ". . . slip through our fingers . . . feel it wisest . . . involvement of . . . Social Services."

There it was. Time reeled back into its regular speed, and I caught up with a rush of blood and terror. "What?" I tried to say, but somehow my lungs didn't have the air. A social worker? One look at the sorry state of our house and I'd be shipped off to a foster home! This couldn't be happening to me. When the Oostermonster kept talking, I took a deep, deep breath and protested. "Hold up! What about the other kids who got taken in that night?"

"Confidentiality forbids me . . ." she began to say.

"What about the two guys who started that fight? Are they having a social worker visit their homes? What about the clowns who vomited on the floor of the police van? Are they getting this attention? What about them? Or is it just Vick Marotti getting slapped in the face? Huh?" While I talked, the vice principal's pen went skittering wildly across her legal pad. I must have been an amateur psychologist's field day. "You can't do this to me!"

"Vickie," said Mrs. Oostergard in her most maddening voice. "If your father . . ."

I'd had it. I was angry, now. "You can stop picking on my dad. He does the best he can." He wasn't going to hear about this conversation, either, that much I knew. I stood up from the chair of inquisition.

"Vickie, would you like a tissue?" Well, glory be. O'Dull *was* awake. He dug into his blazer pocket and pulled out a crumpled travel pack of Kleenex, discarded a used one tucked into its opening, and held it out. A whole world of *ew* wasn't enough!

"There's nothing wrong with having to ask for help, you know." The Oostermonster pushed up her reading glasses. "Do sit down."

"You should be asking for help in reading that police . . . thing . . . you have, because I was *not* arrested and I *hadn't* been drinking." If anything, the cops had thought I was a lot of fun, after they'd realized I wasn't the beeraholic they'd originally suspected, and I showed them a few disappearing-badge tricks while I'd been waiting for my dad. "I've had enough. Thank you for totally wasting my lunch period."

I was already on my feet. All that remained was for me to march over to the door, yank it open, and walk out. Right before it slammed behind me, I heard Mrs. Oostergard's plaintive moo: "Now, Vickie, running away from our problems is never the . . ."

Hah. It might not be the answer, but it sure felt good.

I wasn't all that surprised to find Addy, Little Tony, and Gio lurking beyond the glass front doors outside the main office complex, peering nervously through. Ever since the events of Saturday night, I'd been more or less surrounded by a little band of compatriots from my arrival at school until nearly bedtime. It reminded me a little of all the hobbits who clumped around Mr. Frodo to make sure he didn't do anything stupid with that ring of his. Addy was my Gandalf. "How bad was it?" she asked, her voice oozing with sympathy.

Oh, fan-tizzly-astic, I wanted to say. *The vice principal wants to have some social worker visit my house and say my dad's unfit so I can be put away in some miserable foster home, because I'm a juvie drunk Sped case.* Instead, I let them pull me down and out of sight onto the steps, which they'd decorated with their various lunches. "Eh," was how I verbalized my woes. There was a whole world of unspoken grief behind that "eh."

Technically, kids weren't supposed to take lunch anywhere but the cafeteria and the lot behind the school, but honor students like Gio and Addy could get away with murder. Me, not so much. "Are you okay?" Gio wanted to know.

Forgotten for the moment was his desertion, Saturday night. Right then, I appreciated his hand on mine. Little Tony's arms resting on my shoulders, from behind? Again, not so much. "Want me to have a word with 'em, sweetcheeks?" he asked.

That was a question I could easily ignore. "It's all total bull," I complained. When Addy offered me half her chicken salad sandwich, I accepted. My lunch was shot, anyway. "To them, everything I do is like, totally tainted. I could save a whole orphanage from a fire and they'd make it seem like I'd lit the match. They see me through mud-colored glasses."

Maybe moved by the bitterness in my voice, Addy offered me her pudding Snack Pack as well. I pushed it back. Tapioca. Too much like snot. "They do seem pretty hard on you," she admitted.

Gio spoke up. "It's my fault. If I'd been there . . ."

". . . You'd have been caught in the spell of my jinx and hauled off to the slammer with me. That's not what you need on your record," I told him.

"Yeah, but at least I would've gotten you out."

Addy seemed more than a little annoyed at that. "We all looked for her," she said for about the seventy-first time in the last four days. "We did!"

"It's okay," I responded, as I had all the other seventy times. "I only wish I could've found my pendant."

"I'll stop by and see if his folks swept it up," Gio assured me. "If I can get in. I hear Brandon's on a tight lockdown, now."

Addy was still upset about the implication she'd not done enough to rescue me. "We got out the front only a half-minute before the police stopped. We thought you'd found another escape route."

"I would've carried you. On my shoulders." Yeah, Tony was definitely one of the two stupid hobbits.

"Those parties are always bad news," Gio said, much to my astonishment. "I told you it wasn't worth going."

Was I hearing right? "You wanted to go!"

"No, I didn't. You did," he countered.

We stared at each other, brows furrowed and confused. "I don't even like those parties!" I said.

"Guys." Addy tried to keep the peace, but it was too late.

"Vick, you were so set on going . . ."

"Only because I thought you wanted me to!"

". . . to prove some kind of point . . ."

"Oh, *please*."

"Are we arguing?"

I drew myself up, stunned. "I don't know. Are we?" It surely sounded as if we were. But why? When I glanced guiltily in Addy's direction, she was biting her lip as if trying to think of a way to turn invisible. "I have to fight too many people already," I said slowly.

"I don't want to have to fight you guys. I don't want to have to fight you," I said softly, for Gio.

"Come on, Tony," I heard Addy whisper. "Let's get going."

"Band isn't for another five minutes," he complained.

"Get up now, and there's a pudding pack in it for you."

I almost gasped when that offer made Tony reluctantly rise and follow Addy back into school. I lost to *tapioca?* I felt so cheap. "Sorry," I apologized to Gio. "I didn't mean to . . . I guess the Oostermonster gets my panties in a twist."

"Is there something you want to talk about?" He sat in silence, waiting for an answer I couldn't give. "Vick. You can tell me anything."

Could I? He kept saying that, but did I believe it? Could I really tell him that I'd checked up on him, the night of the party? I felt ashamed to have taken that step. My silence was as good as an *I'll pass*. "I know."

"Has something changed between us?" Oh, no. He was verbalizing the questions I didn't want to ask. Why, Gio? Why? "Lately it feels like things are different."

"Things *are* different," I said, trying to be brisk. I stared at the pavement while I talked. "I'm not doing the witch act anymore, and you're not my producer. It's us all by ourselves now. Maybe that's not . . ." I hadn't wanted to say these words, ever, but here we were. "Maybe that's not enough."

"For you?"

"No!" I said, the words coming out strangled. "For you!"

"Because if there's something missing I'm not giving . . ."

"You!" I could see the headline: GIRL HAS APOPLEXY ON SCHOOL STEPS. "You're what's missing, Gio! I can't be a couple by myself!" From inside the clamor of the first bell rang out, followed by the hubbub of doors opening and people filling the hallways. I didn't want to retread this same old argument. "I've got to go."

He grabbed my hand. "That's only short-term. We'll be back to normal soon."

"When?" I insisted. I didn't wait for an answer. While Gio spluttered out words I knew I'd heard time after time, I hauled myself up and brushed off my butt. "I can't be late for class."

"Is this a break-up?" he asked, scrambling to his feet. "I don't want to break up with you."

The pain that question caused me! Every word was a thin blade to my heart. "No," I told him. I'd broken up with Gio once before, the previous spring, when I'd worried that associating with me might cause colleges to think twice about admitting him. I'd cried afterward for days, behind closed doors. Back then, he'd done nothing to deserve the hurt and confusion I'd caused. Now, though? I wasn't so sure. "It's not a break up. It's a wake-up."

"Vick. No. I'll take tonight off. We can do something."

"Sorry," I said, willing myself not to cave. I had to keep strong. "I'm busy tonight."

And with that, I marched inside the school. Oh, my last three words had been a total, massive lie—but how satisfying it had been, for a change, to be the one saying them.

Was I a total witch? Last year I'd pretended to be one of the magic-working variety. This year I'd given up the smoke and mirrors, but I didn't know. Maybe all that fake darkness couldn't be washed away. Or was I beating myself up over nothing? Was it really so bad to want a boyfriend who actually, you know, paid attention to you?

If there was a clear line between being a kick-me and a total witch, I wanted to know how to walk it.

I'd made it as far as the spot in the school's middle where the central hallway split, leading to the art rooms and wood shop to the right, and the science wing over to the left, when a hand reached out and yanked me into an alcove. Last semester, a wooden bead hanging had kind of occupied that spot until it met a slobbery end, thanks to Rambo the Killer Mountain Goat. They'd never really figured out anything to replace it. "Hey, Marotti," said Tyler. "I was looking for you."

"I don't have time," I said, more sad than hostile. "They'll have my butt on a plate if I'm late."

"There's a couple minutes left still. You missed social studies again." He shrugged. "I was kind of worried."

"No need to worry about Marotti," I joked. "She's made of Teflon. Everything slides right off, huh?"

Okay, it was a lame joke. Neither of us quite bought

131

the bravado behind it. He leaned into the alcove's corner, blinking at me, his long, lean face dead serious. "So who was keeping you? Oostergard or O'Doul?"

"I got the Peking special. One from Column A, one from Column B. Both," I explained.

"Yeah, I got that." Obviously Tyler had no intentions of letting me get away with the corny quips. "Bad, huh?"

Hardly anyone in the stream of kids turned their heads when they passed us; everyone was too busy readying themselves for the next period, shifting backpacks from one shoulder to the other, or digging in their bags for pens and notebooks. "Yeah," I admitted, looking him right in the eyes. "It was pretty bad. Did they—talk to you too?" I asked, suddenly curious.

"Nah."

Instantly I was embarrassed at having asked. I mean, why should I have assumed? "Sorry. Stupid question. You're probably all like, *Why's she asking me that? Just because we've both been on the . . . on the free lunch line?* Rude. Sorry."

"Nope, I wasn't thinking that at all." He crossed his arms. "I mean, my mom wasn't wild about having to pick me up from the station. She had our church minister come by the next afternoon to drop a few verses my way." He grinned a little, let his eyes wander, and looked sheepish. "It was pretty lame."

"Sorry." I winced in sympathy.

"Anyway. I've got notes if you need 'em. Maybe I could drop by your place later, or you could come to mine, or . . ." Okay, that was a little awkward—for the both of us, apparently. He shifted weight. "That sounds kind of weird. Maybe we can look for each other after sixth period, and I can give them to you. She covered the writing of the Constitution. Maybe you already know it all, so . . . okay. I've overstayed my welcome. Later."

"Hey," I told him. My turn to reach out and grab him by the elbow before he slithered away. I'd made a decision during his rambling monologue: Tyler really wasn't that bad a guy. This wasn't the first or even the second or third time he'd gone out of his way to look out for me. He didn't have to. Yet he did. "My place isn't fancy or anything. No billiard room."

He shrugged. "That's cool. I don't play."

"No marble bathtubs. No manicured lawn." He rolled his hands in a *what's your point?* gesture. "With my dad lately, it's a definite mess, too. Not like, used underwear in the living room mess. More like, piles of newspapers and old work stuff he needs to throw out, all over the place mess. But if you want to come over tonight to study some . . . I could use the notes."

As he nodded, the second bell rang. If I timed it right, I could still scamper down the hall and make it to class only a few seconds late—tardy enough to merit a raised eyebrow from the teacher, but not enough for a tick in the wrong column of the attendance book. "You'd better go."

"Later," I said, breaking into a trot. When I looked back, he was staring at me over his shoulder, too. *Boom!* He collided with some freshman kid and nearly careened into the water fountain. Being tall and lanky didn't automatically give a guy grace, I guessed. The doof.

So I hadn't lied to Gio, had I? I was busy tonight, after all.

Pity that the guilt left a sour taste in my mouth, like the bitterest lemon that ever grew.

CHAPTER EIGHT

"Okay, you know I disapprove of all this on principle, don't you?" Addy, very prim and proper, perched on the edge of the concrete bench with her knees pinched together nearly as tightly as her lips. She sounded exactly like her mother.

"Yes, Mrs. Kornwolf," I sighed. Where was Ray? He had promised to pick up the both of us promptly at three-forty. If he didn't arrive immediately, this plan of mine was going to be shot.

"I can't *believe* you called the senior center and pretended to be Gio's mom."

"Yes, Mrs. Kornwolf." I looked at my watch and hopped up and down on the school parking lot curb, a few feet ahead of her. I was freezing. The afternoon was seriously frosty, and mittens were not, and never would be, part of my overall image.

"Worse, you didn't tell *me* about it!"

"No, Mrs. Kornwolf," I muttered. Then, suddenly interested, I asked, "Hey. If you disapprove so much, why are you coming with me today?"

She sniffed. Wisps of vapor streamed from her nostrils as she thought about it. "I felt I owed it to myself to see with my own eyes. That's all."

Ah. Another dead cat, courtesy of curiosity. "You couldn't resist a little sleuthing with your best buddy, admit it."

"Keep dreaming, Nancy Drew."

Tired of sitting, Addy stood up and joined me at the curb. I looked over her outfit once more. "I thought I told you to dress to blend in." Addy wore a knee-length purple and pink nubby overcoat with turquoise buttons, a matching wool cap, and to top it off, dark purple sunglasses with hot pink frames.

"I did!" She looked over first her outfit and then my all-black ensemble as if not seeing much difference.

"What in heck are you planning to blend into? A Barney the Dinosaur video?"

She ignored me. "Here's Ray." Sure enough, Ray's mom's Honda was turning into the driveway, lurching across the student parking lot and circling the cars still remaining until it finally rounded the drop-off point behind Pop Alley, where we'd been waiting for twenty minutes.

"About time." At the lot's far end, as usual parked away from any other cars so it couldn't be accidentally scratched, sat my boyfriend's blue Mustang. "Gio's done with Key Club any minute now."

"I never really understood the Key Club mystique," Addy said. "Everyone in it is always so . . . uptight."

I pinched my nose and announced, "Paging Ms. Pot, paging Ms. Pot, emergency call from Mr. Kettle, white courtesy telephone, please." When her lips pouted in an attempt not to laugh, I said, "Of all people, you know colleges want well-rounded people."

"Yeah, but . . ." Addy stopped talking when the car finally pulled to a halt in front of us. "Hey. Who's . . . ?"

I'd been about to ask the same question. Who? Some unknown person sat in the front seat of the Honda. Hadn't I made it clear that this was a three-person affair? I didn't appreciate Ray dragging along some total stranger. The passenger-side window rolled down, revealing a Goth chick with bruises for eyes and a dark slice of a mouth. Ray leaned past her and said, "Hey guys. Sorry I'm late. Made an extra stop. Vick might want to ride in front," he added to the girl.

"Whatever," she growled, opening the door.

Both Addy and I leapt back on the curb when the girl uncurled from the seat and got out. There was something really familiar about the face, but—I didn't quite know. Strange. She had hair the color of night that looked like it hadn't been combed in about a week. Those smudgy eyes were almost as dark, surrounded by a fingertip-wipe of kohl. Had she made out with a bucket of crude oil? Her lips surely looked it.

And then there were the slumped shoulders, the sloppy black hoodie, the sullen way she stared at the afternoon sky and thrust both hands in the pockets of her oversized black boy's pants. What a freakin' mess. I was startled when Addy spoke up and said, "Oh, my God. Tabitha?"

Holy cannoli! That mess was *Tabitha*? She and I stared at each other, me gaping, she bored, for what felt like a full minute. At last she parted the blotch of a mouth and sighed, "Ray said you wouldn't care."

"Oh, my God," Addy repeated, looking first at Tabitha and then at me. "Freaky."

I shrugged. Tabitha Hunter wasn't someone I'd have picked to come along on this trip, but if she and Ray were gelling, I could deal. "Sure. Whatever."

"You want the front?" she asked.

And stick her in the back with poor Addy? I didn't think so. "You can have it."

She shrugged. "Sure. Whatever."

"Oh, my God!" Addy whispered for a third time. What in the world was her problem? Addy was never the rude type before. She shook her head as if trying to get rid of a bad dream and stumbled around the other side of the Honda. Once we had both stuffed ourselves in the cramped backseat, I found Addy once more mouthing at me, *Oh, my God!* What she said aloud, though, was, "Seat belts!"

While I fastened, Ray looked back and asked, "What's the plan?"

"Pull over there," I told him, gesturing to the corner of the lot closest to the school, but far from any of its exits. "Somewhere we can see the Mustang," I added. From the front passenger seat, Tabitha sighed as if I was in the middle of reading aloud the entire phone book and she couldn't wait until one of us keeled over dead.

"Cloak and dagger stuff, huh?"

"She's been watching too many James Bond movies," Addy grumbled.

Ray leapt right on that tangent. "*Goldfinger* rules."

"I kind of liked *The World Is Not Enough*."

"Not bad. Not classic Bond, but not bad. What do you think?" Ray asked Tabitha.

Her eloquent answer? "Whatever." I was glad she didn't forget the inevitable shrug. That would've been a grievous oversight.

"Guys?" I cleared my throat.

"Anybody bring anything to eat?" Ray wanted to know, stopping the car near the Dumpster. We had a perfect view of both the back cafeteria exit and the Mustang.

"I might have some Cheese Nips from lunch." Addy began digging in her bag.

"Um, guys?" I repeated. This excursion was serious business for me—not a movie club or a picnic. I'd stepped onto thin ice and wanted to make it safely to the other shore. "Can we focus, here?" For once, Tabitha's sigh matched my feelings exactly. "We're supposed to be doing a little recon, not . . ."

"Recon?" Tabitha interrupted, her voice heavy with scorn. "Isn't that like, rat poison?"

Ray had the sense to stay quiet. Addy and I gave each other a certain look. "Actually," Addy said finally, "that's D-con."

"There he is." Ray's hand shot up and forward, pointing to a group of kids leaving the building.

Simultaneously, Addy and Tabitha and I all jerked out our arms to pull his down. My reflexes were quickest, but I sat the farthest away from him. It was Tabitha who was first successful. "Obvious is *so* not pretty." It sounded a lot like something I might say.

"Yeah, don't draw attention, Ray." Addy leaned over and murmured into his ear. "The key to successful reconnaissance is to lay low and not give any indication of what you're doing."

"How do you know so much about it?" Ray slumped down in his seat so that little of his forehead remained visible over the steering wheel.

"It's common sense. Haven't you ever followed anyone before?"

Ray moaned and slid down farther. "I'm in a car filled with professional stalkers."

"Oh, come off it. Vick, what do we do now? Vick?" Addy shook my arm.

I shushed her. I'd been listening, but all my attention had been on Gio. As usual, he was grinning from ear to ear, probably at some joke one of the other Key Club clowns had made. I felt ashamed. I used to crave that smile. I still did. How could I have fallen so low as to spy on my own boyfriend? Did anyone really do that kind of thing? Anyone who wasn't on some bad soap on the WB, anyway? A long time ago I'd kind of come to terms with the fact that I wasn't *normal*, that I'd never really quite fit in. But I'd never given up on the feeling that normal or not, at least as a person I was still *decent*.

What I'd initiated that afternoon wasn't what decent people did. Not by a long shot. If I followed through, I might never reclaim that decent feeling again. How could I suspect him of lying to me? Anyone could look at Gio and see he was a good kid. He was the center of attention with those Key Club kids; they all listened to what he said as he waved goodbye, and watched as he strolled casually to the parking lot.

Having a group break up the minute you depart—that's what true popularity is, and Gio had it. A couple of girls followed him while the rest of the crowd scattered to their cars and bikes. I didn't know either of them. All I could really think of was what Tyler had said to me the week before. He was right. I might not have known those girls' names, but they probably knew mine.

"You seriously think he could be seeing one of those Barbies?" Ray asked.

"No." Could I sound any more annoyed? Doubtful. "I don't think he's . . . crud. I don't know."

If I couldn't get my own words out, how could anyone else guess what I was trying to say? "What's the deal?" Tabitha wanted to know. "Carson's hooking up with somebody?"

"We don't know that." Good old Addy, always leaping to my defense.

Tabitha's sigh shook the car like a magnitude 4.5 earthquake. "Drama!"

"It's not my imagination!" I protested. Gio waved a final farewell to the girls and, with a jaunty little skip in his step, sprinted in the direction of his car. I could have sworn he was probably whistling. "He's been different, lately."

"I don't know about that," said Addy, who seemed torn between maintaining her dark-lensed disguise and being actually able to see anything.

Ray watched her lift and drop her shades in the rearview mirror. "No, Vick's right. He has been different." I admit I was surprised at the unexpected support. "I don't know that it's hooking up or anything, but he's been acting weird lately. Not as together in English, either. He used to be real on top of everything."

By the Mustang's side, Gio popped open the back and tossed in his book bag. His hand seemed to linger a moment or two too long on the reef blue paint as he shut it again. He'd almost given it a caress. I remembered a time he used to run his hand over my trunk like that.

Or something. That didn't come out quite right.

Could I be jealous? Of his *car?* Maybe I was insane, after all. "There he goes," Addy said when Gio opened the driver's side. His arm swung loosely as the door heaved back. He looked like an old-fashioned guy inviting some dressed-up chick to waltz. Then, after looking around to see if anyone in the immediate vicinity was observing, he brushed some probably-imaginary dust off the freshly washed finish, leapt into the air, then jumped in, narrowly avoiding banging his head in the process. Ooch. The door shut.

Were we all holding our breath, waiting for him to drive away? If so, there was a good chance we were going blue in the face. From our distance, it wasn't easy to see what was going on inside—all I could really make out from Gio's silhouette was that he leaned over, as if retrieving something from the floor or glove compartment, then straightened back up. In the Honda, the only sounds were the creak of Ray's leather coat against the vinyl seats, Tabitha's occasional huffing, and Addy's attempts to crane her neck to see better.

"What in the world?" she mumbled.

My question exactly. The Mustang bounced up and down slightly, still parked at an angle in the lot's farthest corner. My boyfriend's head jerked back and forth, thrashing wildly. Was Gio having some kind of fit? Did he need help? After a minute of watching the car's heavy frame bound and rebound on its shocks, Ray eased down his window an inch. Very, very distantly, we could all hear a muffled sound of drums and bass. "Dude likes his air guitar," Ray said at last. Addy snorted.

I wasn't deterred. After all, how long could a guy sit in his own car and rock out?

From 3:45 until 4:05, apparently. And hoo boy, was it one of the longest twenty minutes of my life. Not because of my impatience, though that was a factor. Mostly because all during the long period Gio sat there bobbing up and down, drumming his hands on the steering wheel, thrashing his head and moving his mouth like he was singing at the top of his voice, I felt embarrassed for him. Everybody does silly stuff like that when they think they're not being watched, right? Nothing shameful in it. Me? Sometimes I'd shut the door to my bedroom, turn my clock radio up, up, way up, and dance around in my socks to made-up routines, just for the energy it lent me. And of course, we all have those moments where, you know, our fingers will do a little Indiana Jones excavation in the ol' nasal caves of doom, when we think nobody's looking.

That's the whole thing, though. We always assume no one's watching during those private moments when we cut loose. Watching Gio pretend he was a one man U2 felt invasive, like spying on him right at the moment his doctor told him to turn his head and cough, or catching him with his pants around his ankles during a gastric emergency. I was a horrible, horrible person. The others, judging by their stunned silence, must have been thinking along similar lines.

Or so I supposed until Ray finally shook his head in awe and commented, "I've got to get that CD."

"He's moving," I announced, forgetting about playing it cool and pointing right at the Mustang. "Start the car."

"I see, I see." Ray turned the ignition and drifted into drive, creeping forward slowly while Gio executed a three-point turn until he faced the exit. "Don't worry. I'll stay back."

"But not *too* far back," I begged. "Let's not lose him."

"Right. Not too far back."

"But not too close, either. Leave some space."

"Right. Leave some space." Ray sounded agreeable enough.

"Watch out in case he spots you and tries to ditch us."

Ray narrowed his eyes. "You're planning on having a high-speed chase?"

"Vick, listen to you!" Addy interrupted. "You sound like a crazy girl. You're a crazy girl saying crazy things. Don't give me that look! You know I'm right. We shouldn't be doing this. We should be going to the mall and getting cheese-on-a-stick or something."

"Mmm." Ray smacked his lips. "Cheese-on-a-stick."

"I have to find out what's going on," I said. Gio's car had reached the end of the school drive, dozens of yards ahead of us. His left turn signal flashed bright red. "If you don't want to come . . ."

"No, I'm in this with you because you're my friend." Why did that reassure me only a little? "And because you asked. I still think we'd be better off at the mall."

"What's it going to be?" Ray called back. We were at the drive's end now ourselves. The Mustang's tail lights were visible at the end of the road.

"Stalk on, MacDuff," I ordered.

Poor Ray. I could tell his regretful mumble was probably for the cheese-on-a-stick we could have been having. "You know, there's a song that says if you love someone, you should set them free," he said.

"What does that *mean*, exactly?" I asked with more than a little irritation. I was getting it from all sides here.

"It's like, you know. If you really love somebody . . . you should, like, set them. . . ."

"Free?" I guessed. "That poet's vocabulary of yours sure comes in handy, huh?"

"Don't be rude to Ray," Addy said, looking out the window. We were a good eighth of a mile behind Gio, I anxiously noted, but the road leading into town was pretty empty for that time of day.

"I think it's like pet birds," Tabitha said suddenly. "You can put them in a cage if you want, but they won't be happy about it. They like it best when they're free, right? And if, you know, they really like you, they won't go flying off if you treat them right. But you never know for sure until you try." She crossed her arms. "Something like that."

Ray smiled over at her from the driver's seat. "That was nice," he decided. Then, to us in the back, he added, "That's what I meant."

Boy, Tabitha must really have taken to heart my advice at the party last week about not going so overboard with Ray. She barely acknowledged his compliment at all. "Sure. Okay."

"And what if they fly off?" I demanded.

She shrugged again and pointed to her cheek. "Tear."

Stealing my line? Irritating. Deeply, deeply irritating. "Who listens to song lyrics, anyway? For everyone's information," I said, "I *am* letting Gio free. At the moment I'm only putting a tracking device on him. He's turning!"

"I see." Ray eased into the left turn lane. "You know, I bet he's going to the comic book store. Should I pull in with him? There's not much parking."

I had to think quickly. The old cluster of shops at the corner was pretty tiny; the only other stores in that strip were a cell phone outlet, a place for dis-

146

count smokes, and some kind of Vietnamese grocery. If we parked on that side of the street, there'd be no way we'd stay out of Gio's sight. "The strip mall across the street. Hurry," I instructed.

"The one with the Starbucks?"

"Hot chocolate!" Addy moaned with deep longing. I glared at her. "Or not."

I could see Gio's blond spikes rising from his car when we drove by on the right side of the street and turned into the fancier strip mall. They'd finished it only a few months ago; the complex not only boasted the sole Starbucks in town, but one of those expensive frozen steak stores and a fancy sandwich shop, too. A lot of the kids made the short trek to this particular corner after school. The trendier ones stuck to this side of the street for their caffeine fixes. The comic book store on the other was Mecca to the geekier ones, I'm afraid. They'd haunt the aisles for their favorite graphic novels and newly released anime. Weird, though. I'd never known Gio to visit that particular store before.

"I'm getting out," Ray announced. Apparently he anticipated my protest, because he cut me off with, "It's my car . . . my mom's . . . and I need to stretch my legs."

You know how they say some people can't chew gum and walk at the same time? Apparently I was totally unable to talk and spy on Gio simultaneously. "Don't . . . go . . . far . . ." The words came out one at a time while I watched the blond head bob toward the comic book store. The head, unfortunately, was all I could see; some SUV blocked my view of the rest of his body, as well as most of his car. I was going to have to keep a close eye on his front grille, if I wanted to keep this up.

When both Ray and Tabitha opened their doors and exited, the cold air from outside invigorated me. Four people in a tiny Honda doesn't exactly make for comfortable breathing. "Drama!" I heard Tabitha say once more, right before she slammed the car shut again.

"Oh. My. God." Addy grabbed hold of my arm and gave each word in her sentence a special emphasis. "What do you think?"

"I don't know. Maybe he's trading in some DVDs or something."

"Hel-lo. Earth to one-track mind. Come in, one-track mind." I blinked, and tore my eyes away from the narrow little storefront across the street. "I'm not talking about Gio. I mean Tabitha. Didn't you notice?"

"Yeah, sure," I said, resuming my watch. "She's gone edgy."

"Edgy?" she nearly screeched.

"Yeah. A little less polish. Rougher around the edges. That kind of thing."

"She's you!"

Addy had my attention now. "She's what? What do you mean, she's me?"

"Look at her!" Ignoring the law of not attracting attention, Addy waved her hand in Tabitha's direction. "She could be your twin!"

"What? Don't be asinine. There's no w—" I gulped. The darker, messier hair. The kohl. The lips. The outfit that made the cast of *The Nightmare Before Christmas* look positively perky in comparison. She really *was* my twin, or at least a sister who looked an awful lot like me. We both had the same kind of heart-shaped face, the big eyes. Hadn't I said "Drama!" or something similar the night of the party disaster? She was totally copying my act! "I'm not *that* sour, am I?" I asked suddenly, panicking when Addy chose to turn her head and study the front window of Starbucks. "Hey! Oh, come on! I'm not!"

"Well," Addy admitted, "She's laying on the sighing and the *whatevers* a little thick."

"I sure hope so."

"If I were casting the movie of your life, though? She'd be hired already."

Impossible! When I looked at the sidewalk, where my twin leaned against the new, red bricks of the coffee shop, I saw Tabitha flick her eyes away from Ray, who had his hand close to her shoulder, supporting his weight against the wall. "Is it some kind of mean joke or something?"

"That *would* be your first explanation, wouldn't it?" I turned my head away from the budding couple and regarded Addy with amazement. "You're so paranoid that people are out to get you. No, she's not mocking. You're popular enough that people are trying to copy you. Maybe not to that extent," she said, waggling a finger at Tabitha. "But they do."

"Weird!" My surprise was total. Somehow, I felt both kind of honored, and yet utterly ashamed. Is that really how people thought I acted? Why had Addy recognized what Tabitha was doing when I hadn't? "But why . . . why is Ray into that? He didn't pay her a lick of attention before."

"Oh, Vick." What? What was I missing this time? Addy shook her head and crossed her arms. Pity was in her voice. "You don't think there's anything significant about the fact that now Tabitha looks like you, Ray is head over heels?"

"No, except . . ." Oh, crud. I saw what she meant, now. "You mean Ray . . . likes . . . me?" I finished weakly. She nodded. "How come I didn't know?"

"Would you have gone out with him?"

"No . . . I mean, I like Ray. As a friend."

She nodded. "That's probably why he never said anything."

"Oh." I fell silent. All I'd wanted was an afternoon's worth of stalking, not a whole world of weirdness. Everything seemed to be changing around me, transforming without me having the slightest say. I admit I'm a control freak. What magician isn't? We like to know and manipulate exactly what people see and think is happening. Only this time, I was the hapless observer in the audience, trying to figure out what led where. It was unsettling. "Should I say . . . ?"

"Gio," Addy interrupted. Sure enough, across the street, I could see Gio's head moving across the parking lot in the direction of his car. She rapped on the Honda's back window to capture Ray's attention. "And no. Don't say a thing."

"I'd be tactful." The look of incredulity she gave me stung. "What? I would!"

"Don't."

I couldn't say another word. Both Ray and Tabitha resumed their seats, bringing the chilly outdoor temperatures with them. "All right," said Ray, starting the car once more and pulling out of the parking lot. "Let's get this party started again."

"He was barely in there for sixty seconds," Addy said.

"Ahhhh, get out my way, you . . . !" Ray let loose with a few choice swear words. A minivan directly in front of us blocked most of the access driveway and had turned on its left blinker. Rush-hour traffic—such as it is in this Podunk city, anyway—had begun to clog the road, and when I looked both ways, it seemed like we were going to be sitting there for a while. Across from us, Gio's Mustang nosed halfway out into the street; he made his own left turn with precious little space between him and an oncoming tow truck.

"He's getting away!" I shouted.

"Keep your eye on him." Ray laid on the horn. The minivan didn't budge. "Aw, lady!"

"Hit her!" I yelled. "Nudge her!"

"Do you have a driver's license?" Ray asked, presumably rhetorically. Everyone knew I didn't, though I knew how to drive. "Then kindly shut up! Nudge her! WTF?" he muttered.

The lights on the Mustang were disappearing fast. "Oh man, we're going to lose him."

"He's going to the senior center," Addy pointed out. "Doesn't his shift start at four-thirty? It's what, a mile down the road?" *If that's where he was going,* I couldn't help but think. "We'll catch up," she assured me.

I wasn't so sure. Every passing second behind the bumper of that stupid minivan felt like an eternity, but at last it edged forward enough that with one wince-inducing flooring of the gas pedal, we squeezed by and out onto the traffic-filled road. "I've lost him," I said.

"Don't worry," Ray assured me. "I've got a plan."

Ray's plan appeared to consist of driving as fast he could, changing lanes whenever he saw a slow-moving car ahead, and running through yellow lights like a maniac. In other words, perfectly ordinary driving, for him. I had to hand it to Tabitha, though; if she was imitating me, she was doing it a lot better than I was. I spent the whole, rushed trip doing exactly what I'd done on the Tower of Terror when I'd visited Disneyland as a kid—clutching onto the seat and trying not to scream my head off. Tabitha, though, pulled out a Whitman's Sampler assortment of sighs, hair tosses, and bored yawns. Dang, but she was one cool chick.

The senior center lay off the broad road past where all the restaurants and shops began to peter out and the town began to fade to countryside, quickie oil change by quickie oil change. I hadn't seen the Mustang for at least a minute and a half by the time we turned onto the quiet by-way, but Ray pointed in the direction of the low, sprawling building when we were within sight. "See?" he said, his voice full of triumph. "I told you we'd catch up."

"You were right," I admitted. "One hundred percent correct." Gio was driving down the center's far driveway, where I suppose a parking lot lay behind the building. A short glimpse was all I was able to get, because within another few seconds it had vanished again.

"Great," Tabitha drawled. "So let me get this

straight. We went to a lot of trouble so we could follow your boyfriend all the way . . . to *work*? Gosh, that was a blast."

Did I talk like that? Did I honestly talk like that? If so, why weren't people smacking me left and right? "Pull in the front," I told Ray, not wanting to have a close encounter of the Gio kind at that awkward moment. It was kind of a come down from all the scenarios I'd been imagining, I had to admit. "We found out a lot of useful things this afternoon, thank you," I told her.

"Like?"

Like you're a total fraud, I thought to myself. Addy might have seen the words about to pop out of my lips, because she said in a consoling tone, "This is exactly where you hoped he'd go, right? So it's a happy ending. And," she added happily, "we still have time for cheese-on-a-stick."

"Or Starbucks," Ray said with longing.

"No." Everyone looked at me as if I were crazy. "Not yet," I told them. "We have to make sure he's actually working."

"Oh, God," sighed Ray.

"Vick." I could tell without looking that Addy was wearing her schoolmarm expression again. "It's been fun. We played spy for a little bit. We followed your boyfriend here. All we found out is that he likes a little private time with his car stereo. Let's call it a day."

"I have to see that he's actually here to volunteer." I didn't care if I sounded stubborn.

"As opposed to what?" Ray said, turning around in his seat. He hadn't shut off the car; it was obvious he wanted to be on his way. "Hanging out at the old folks' home so he can fleece retirees at Texas hold 'em?"

"I don't want to stalk him through the corridors, thank you very much. All I want is someone to tell me he's working," I repeated. "I know it sounds lame. You don't have to come with. I'll go in, find the desk . . ." How could I explain to them that I couldn't simply trust the evidence of my eyes? I knew too well they could be fooled. My heart had to believe as well.

"You are so not going in there." Addy's announce-ment made me bristle, but I calmed down at what was to follow. "I'll go. If you walk in the way you are now, nostrils flaring and whatnot, there'll be a scene. So let me." When I didn't object, she started to un-buckle her seat belt. "I'll be discreet. He'll never know we were here. Then we can go out for hot chocolate and pretend none of this ever happened."

"Riiiiight," said Ray. "*You'll* be discreet!"

"Why wouldn't I?"

In his husky voice, Ray said, "In that purple thing? What's Gio going to think when he hears some copper-headed girl with a grape Kool-Aid coat came looking for him? He'll know it's you."

"Exactly. Thank you, Ray, for pointing out the flaws in Addy's plan!" I loosened my own belt. "I won't take lo—"

"That's why I'll go." I sat back, exasperated beyond words. "I'm a dude. If they say anything like, *Hey, Gio, someone came looking for you*, and he says *Oh yeah, who?*, all they'll say is, *Some dude.*" His seat buckle slid back. "So that's settled."

"Settled, my precious rear end!" I protested. My friend's plans had more holes than Tabitha's fishnets.

Ray, however, was already out of the car. We'd parked in the semi-circular drive in front of the building's main entrance. "We won't be longer than fifteen minutes, right?" he asked, pointing to a short-term parking sign next to us.

"No way," said Addy.

"I'll be quick," Ray said before he shut the door, more for Tabitha than anyone else.

"Whatever," said my evil clone, watching him stroll away.

We all sat in silence until Ray disappeared through the front doors. Despite the fact Addy had been ragging on me about this stupid excursion since it started—or maybe *because* she'd been ragging on me—I felt compelled to apologize. "I know you think I'm crazy," I said softly, so I didn't feel we were being eavesdropped on by an even crazier girl. "Maybe I am. I've had this odd, odd feeling that Gio's not telling me something."

"So what? Do you tell him everything? I mean, everything?" What was she getting at? An enormous lump filled my throat right then, a lump of unadulterated guilt. Did she know that Tyler had been over to my house three times that week? Or was she talking about one of the other zillion things I kept to myself? "It's frustrating. I want you guys to work out. I thought you were working out. I really don't understand why we're doing this."

The lump in my throat plummeted straight into my gut. Addy couldn't know about Tyler's visits. It wasn't as if he and I had done anything wrong, anyway. Homework and talking and some TV were about the extent of it. Physical contact? There hadn't been any. I hadn't so much as shaken his hand. But what if someone found out and told Gio? Would he give me any more benefit of the doubt than I had him?

I didn't say anything, though. I sat quietly and listened to the hum and sputter of the car's motor.

It was Tabitha who broke the silence. "Here he comes."

Naturally I assumed she meant Ray. The sidewalk was empty. To my surprise, though, a reef blue Mustang blew down the side drive from the building's back, speeding in the direction of the road. All three of our heads swiveled as it flew by not ten yards from us, our mouths rounded into identical O's.

"Holy . . . !" I whispered.

"Um." Addy gulped.

"Should I get Ray?" Tabitha wanted to know.

"No time." I made an executive decision. Lightning-quick, I was out the back door and around the car and in the driver's seat. My heard thudded. Could I do this? I was pretty sure I could. Over both Addy's and Tabitha's shrieked protests, I shifted into drive. Or rather, what I thought was drive, but really was reverse. "Oops," I muttered after we lurched backwards.

"Don't you *dare!* Get out of that seat this minute!" Addy screamed directly into my ear.

Finally we lurched forward. "Hang on, guys," I called out, as we swerved around a surprised mail truck. "This ride might get a little bumpy!"

CHAPTER NINE

"Don't engage." From the backseat, Addy attempted to keep her voice steady, pleasant, and conversational, as if the police officers in the car next to ours might be listening. Never mind that our windows were completely rolled up, and that with her mouth a foot and a half from my ear, even I could barely hear her. "Don't look over. Don't look guilty. Act natural."

I glanced back in the rearview mirror. "Are they staring our way?"

Tabitha leaned forward in her seat. "The driver is, kind of. Now he's not. Now he is."

"*Don't!*" Addy snapped. "Don't call any attention to us! If we get pulled over and they find out Vick doesn't have a license . . ."

"They're not going to pull us over. I'm not doing anything wrong."

"Other than carjacking?"

I made a face. "I meant, right *now*."

"Your luck hasn't been so great lately. I'm just saying."

I felt a flush spread from my chest and underarms, radiating out to my limbs. Addy's flat statement had tied my stomach in knots. Hopping into the driver's seat had seemed like a dandy solution—the only solution—two minutes before. Now, though, I was being attacked by all kinds of doubt and shame and regret. When the police car had pulled up in the lane next to mine at the stoplight, I'd worried that Ray had sent them. Then I'd worried they'd maybe seen me speeding, though I hadn't been going faster than any other car on the busy road. I'd worked myself up to a paranoid fantasy that they'd been following my every move since the night of the party and was envisioning my daily prison routine when Tabitha said, "Why don't you have a license, anyway?"

At least that was an issue I could address honestly. "Because I haven't taken the test, yet." My jaw barely moved. I didn't feel compelled to mention the fact that my dad couldn't have afforded car insurance for me if I'd wanted my license, anyway. We didn't need quite that much honesty.

"So how do you know how?"

"Gio taught me." Over the summer, in the very car we pursued, two lights ahead. "Are they still watching?"

"*Don't look!*" Boy, all I can say is that if the U.S. military needs a few good drill sergeants, they might want to start recruiting in the Millard Fillmore High School junior class. At Addy's bark, I froze. I would've dropped into push-up position right in the middle of traffic if she'd ordered it. "Just smile. Pretend you're having fun."

"But I'm not," I said, through a fake jack o' lantern grin.

"*Pretend*," she all but screamed. Then she followed up by laughing her head off, like one of us had told a funny joke. "Oh, God, why am I here?"

I jumped at an unexpected sound that seemed to have been scientifically formulated to startle me out of my skin. For the two seconds it took my armpits to destroy completely the deodorant I'd applied that morning, my brain decided it was a police siren. Yet when Tabitha began digging into her jacket pocket, I realized it was merely a cell phone with an unusually annoying ring. "Hey," she said flatly into the tiny little thing. "Where are you?"

"The light's changing," I announced. At last! In the distance, though my view had been mostly blocked by afternoon traffic, I watched as Gio's light switched from red to green, and then as the signal between us followed suit. A few seconds later, our light blinked, too. "Watch the cops."

"We're kind of . . . moving the car," Tabitha said, looking to me for approval. "No, we didn't get a ticket. Why . . . ? Oh. It's Ray," she told us, nervously covering the little microphone. *No kidding, Einstein!* "He heard you say something about the cops."

"Everything's fine!" I shouted in the phone's direction as I stepped on the gas.

"Don't tell him everything's fine. You tell people everything's fine when everything's not fine," Addy muttered.

"Are you watching the cop car?" I asked her.

"Yes! They're getting in the left turn lane." Somehow I got the impression that Addy might have been happier right then if I was being hauled away in cuffs. Not that I really could blame her—after all, I'd broken any number of rules by that point. I craned my neck and saw the black-and-gold squad car in the middle of the road, turn signal blinking. False alarm. For now, anyway.

"Ray says he wants to talk to you."

I regarded Tabitha's phone like it was the hand of some guy who'd moments before bragged that he never washed his hands after taking a leak. All my driver's education, such as it was, had taken place either in the school parking lot during the deserted summer months, the Arcadia Mall lot on Sundays, or twice on the real roads during early weekend mornings when the traffic had consisted mostly of me and a couple of delivery vans with yawning drivers. There'd been plenty of space for me on all four sides. Sitting in a steady stream of cars in stop-and-go conditions was making my palms sweat so badly that I already could barely hold on to the steering wheel. Now I was supposed to talk on the phone at the same time? Crispy critters! You might as well ask me to work crossword puzzles and whistle opera on top of all the steering and pedaling and signal-flipping I was already responsible for! "I can't. I kinda, sorta, can't," I babbled, hoping they didn't notice when I came close to nudging a newspaper truck.

I must've looked as panicked as I felt. "I'll put him on speakerphone," she said, hitting a button.

"Hey, where are you guys?" Oh, how I dreaded hearing that trusting, cheerfully gruff voice. Especially when I knew how in a matter of seconds, it would change forever.

"Around the corner?" I improvised, stalling for time. Around the corner and a mile down the road. Technically not a lie, right?

"Oh, he is so going to kill you," I heard from the backseat.

From the tinny little speaker, Ray's voice said, "What did she say? Kill what?"

"Addy was saying she's *thrilled* you called." I didn't care if taking my eyes off the road for a split second meant possibly shearing off a side-view mirror. I had to whip around and give a certain somebody the stink-eye. "So you didn't find Gio, huh?"

"No, I did. He's here." Ray sounded positively gleeful. "I mean, I didn't see him or anything. They said he'd checked in and gone to the clinic to help one of the nurses. Then the receptionist started raving about how everyone loved their little Gio. Kind of sickening." Maybe I hadn't heard right? I refocused on the road as we drove past the Starbucks once again. "You there?" I heard.

"Ray? That's kind of impossible." I gulped and bit the bullet. Every second was taking us farther and farther away from the senior center. Up ahead, the Mustang pulled into the right-hand lane. "We all saw Gio drive away like, right after you went in."

"Nuh-uh!"

"Yuh-huh."

"Nuh-uh!" I was all ready with another *yuh-huh* when he added, "You must've seen someone else, V. The women were all totally sure their adorable little

Gio was down in the clinic. One of the women hanging around told me he'd pushed her to the desk when he came in. She told him some really long story about a pumpkin pie recipe she lost and he told her . . ."

What was happening? Gio couldn't be in two places at once. Things .were getting weirder and weirder. I tuned out the fascinating pumpkin pie story and worked out the possibilities in my head:

1) The Mustang wasn't Gio's. But let's face facts. How many three-year-old reef blue Mustangs were hanging around the parking lot of the senior center? So maybe . . .

2) Whoever was driving the Mustang wasn't Gio. He could've lent it to, oh, I don't know. The guy who calls bingo numbers on Wednesday afternoons. Considering how that car was his baby, though, the lending scenario was about as likely as me getting a sudden yen to run for prom queen.

So I was left with the possibility that:

3) My boyfriend had cloned himself in the school bio lab so that he could double the number of extracurricular activities that would appear on his college applications. If that was true? Ew. Had I been kissing up on the clone or the real thing?

". . . you still there?" I heard Ray say. He'd finished the pumpkin pie story and was repeating the question, I realized. Between thinking and following and driving, I'd lost track. "Where are you guys anyway? I walked around to the back and I don't see you anywhere. Honk or something."

"You might not hear if I honk right now," I hedged, right as Addy let out a peal of bitter laughter in the background.

"Why not? Where did you park?"

"Not *too* far away."

"You know the Melody Diner?" Tabitha asked, right as we passed the old silver-and-white eatery and turned onto the parkway around the city courthouse.

I could have killed the wench. "She's joking!" I yelled. Now that we were on a smaller road, there was less traffic. I could see the Mustang clearly, only a block ahead.

"The only Melody I know is the one in the middle of . . . hey. No. Vick? Vick, what're you up to?"

I couldn't answer. To Tabitha I tried mouthing the words *Turn it off! Turn it off!*, but she misunderstood. "Are you telling me to *hmmm* off?" she asked, glaring. I guessed that despite all the neo-Goth trappings, she still had a thing about four-letter words. "Rude!"

"No!"

"You . . . *took* . . . *my* . . . *car?*" None of us answered. "Who's driving?"

Thank God. Another stoplight. Thinking quickly, I gargled to mimic static. "*Khhhhh* bad signal *kkkkhh-hhh* breaking up *kkkkkhhhhhhh* have to *kkhh* later.*"

Ray's voice, however, was loud and clear. The last words we heard him say, right before I snatched the cell phone out of Tabitha's black-nailed little hands and started pressing buttons at random, were, "Vick, that trick doesn't even work in the *movies*—!" The phone's display winked out.

"You might leave that off for a while," I suggested, tucking the phone in the cup holder.

"Rude!" Tabitha commented. On the plus side, she really didn't look any grumpier than she had before I stole her boyfriend's car.

We were driving through one of the city's nicer residential areas now, where lawyers and doctor's houses mingled with professors from the local college and professionals who worked in the stamp-sized downtown area. Last year, my dad and I had driven through these same streets after dark to look at the Christmas lights. Now, though, I didn't at all notice the big brick houses or the spacious front yards; my whole world was the length of the six cars between me and Gio. Where was he going?

I heard the chirp of Addy's phone behind me. That would be Ray—who else could it be? "I'm answering it." Addy sounded firm. Defiant, even. In any other little melodrama, I'd have been proud of her for standing up to the villain of the piece . . . but of course, I was the mustache-twiddler here. I was going to have to spend weeks, if not longer, getting back in everyone's good graces after this. What mattered now, though, was keeping up.

"Fine," I told her. "Do whatever."

"Hello?" I heard her say. "Yes, everything's okay." Her voice dropped to a low volume; she covered her mouth. Whatever. I didn't need the distraction.

Where was Gio going? At the edge of the neighborhood, where the divided street dead-ended onto another main thoroughfare, Gio turned and headed north. We were less than a mile from the mall now, driving along a street lined with donut shops and garden supply stores and video rental places and, half a mile ahead of us, the burg's only Wal-Mart. It was a part of town people visited when they wanted a quick bite or had something to buy . . . or several somethings, since nearly every kind of mainstream chain store lurked somewhere in the area. Since I didn't usually have pocket change to spare, it wasn't really very often I'd found myself wandering these particular streets.

At least the road was broader here—four lanes on either side of the divider, and wide enough that I could easily spy Gio darting around traffic as he zoomed to the west. "Ray says he's not mad," Addy announced, then immediately contradicted herself into the phone. "Oh, come on. You're not. No," she told him. "But he wants his mom's car back. How much farther are we going?"

How could I answer? It wasn't a matter of setting an egg timer and turning around when it dinged. Didn't they know the situation was distressing me as much as it was them? Maybe not. I accelerated through a yellow light in silence before answering. "Tell Ray I'm really, really, really sorry," I called back. "And tell him . . . tell him . . . crud!"

"That's not much of a message."

Addy was right, but I wasn't talking to her. I'd lost sight of the Mustang. Another wave of panic set in. What the hell was I going to do now? "He's gone," I announced. If I tore my hair out, would anyone at school mistake it for the newest and hottest style?

"No, he turned in right there." Tabitha extended her hand toward a driveway not far from us.

"Why didn't you say something?"

"I thought you saw!" she grumped. "If you don't talk, I can't read your mind!"

Way to overreact, Vick. "Sorry."

"Ray says he'll be in trouble if he's not home by dinner."

"Aren't you like, paying for every second you talk to him?" I asked, turning in the drive.

"I've got rollover minutes." From her tone, I guessed Addy wished I was the one getting rolled over.

"There." Tabitha pointed again. We'd pulled into a shopping center anchored by one of those hardware superstores at one end, and a giant pet supply superstore at the other. Between them lay a bunch of much smaller shops, less super, by which Gio sped. He turned into an alley midway down, and disappeared once more.

This was it, I felt certain. Where else was there for him to run? The area behind the complex was walled up—a veritable dead end for all of us. I could see only stacks of cardboard boxes ready for recycling, some dumpsters, and an abandoned trailer propped up on a leg where the truck should have been, to one side. Down a few dozen feet on the other side, parked among a number of other cars, the Mustang had finally come to a stop.

Ignoring the NO PARKING sign on the driveway curb, I pulled over. "I'm going on my own from here," I told my two kidnapping victims. "Wait for me, okay?"

"Sure beans," said Addy. "Like you waited for Ray?"

"Addy . . ." She was angry, I knew. I got it, okay? Tabitha didn't seem any too happy with me, either, though what with her new Vick-style makeover, it was really difficult to tell what she was really thinking. "Do what you have to do. Okay?" I'd decided to leave the decisions to her, for a change. "You have my total and utter permission."

The car was so warm that I'd nearly forgotten how frigid it was when I climbed outside. I'd scarcely closed the door when I heard another latch click. Addy stepped out beside me, shaking loose her long, red hair. She still clutched the cell phone, though she'd disconnected from Ray. Was she going to lecture me once more? I could probably recite my faults with her from memory, now.

We looked at each other in silence for a few seconds. I was about to turn and leave when at last her lips opened. "We'll wait," she finally whispered. "Try not to be too long. Okay?"

I nodded. "Fair enough." It was as close to a blessing as I'd get from her at that point. Before she opened the door and lowered herself into the driver's seat, though, Addy put her hand on my sleeve and gave my arm a squeeze.

I liked that. The gesture gave me courage enough to walk around the corner, into the alley. From the back, it was impossible to guess what kind of stores the doors belonged to—all that distinguished the rear doors were sticky-backed reflective address numbers gleaming from each.

The sound of a creaking door on its hinges sent me scurrying behind the nearest of the Dumpsters set at regular intervals beside each of the shop's rear entries. The noises sounded more like a sound effect from a haunted house movie than something you'd hear in the heart of commercial suburbia. Near where the Mustang was parked, I heard voices.

It was easy enough to tiptoe to the next Dumpster—no one could see me. I cocked my head and listened. "... Yeah, probably a busy shift," I heard an older man say with one of those raspy voices that comes from serious abuse of cigarettes. "And Mark's out again, so I'm short one team tonight. Think you can stay 'til nine again?"

"Yeah." I held my breath. That was Gio speaking. "Sure. No problem. I could use the extra cash."

The sour reek of burning tobacco tickled my nose from the other side of the Dumpster. Whoever the older guy was must have been stubbing out the last of a smoke, because I heard the crunch of a shoe sole on the asphalt. "Wife says I ought to give the things up. Hard habit to break, though. You okay going out with Shelley tonight?"

Who was this Shelley? "Yeah." What was I listening for in Gio's voice? Would I recognize betrayal if I heard it? "Sure."

"She's a good kid. She looks up to you. All right. Let's go in. I've already got a couple of deliveries ready." I held my breath while footsteps passed not six feet from me. Then the door creaked again. I waited for a moment, but heard nothing. I was alone.

So. An hour's worth of stalking and what had I found? I felt as if I'd sat in on a game of poker and had been dealt a hand of blank cards. It surely meant something, but I wasn't entirely sure what. Was Gio involved in some kind of shady doings? Was that what the delivery was? Or was I being overwrought and paranoid again? After all, most shopping centers didn't exactly harbor storefronts for drugs or counterfeit artwork tucked in between their Sew Prettys and their Baby Gaps.

I crept out from behind the Dumpster and approached the brown door, which had been left slightly ajar. All I wanted was a quick peek inside. I'd catch an eyeful, then scoot back to the car and try to figure it all out. That was my intention, anyway. What happened is that when I got next to the door, it swung open and nearly hit me square in the face. I jumped back into the shadows by the wall, feeling like a cheese-seeking mouse caught in the middle of a kitchen in broad daylight with hungry cats on every side and nowhere to run. "We'll take care of the west side delivery first," Gio said in a matter-of-fact voice as he walked toward his car. Though his back was to me, I could see his arms were full with flat boxes. Gone were the blue jeans and red henley he'd been wearing when he came out of school earlier. Now he wore black 501s and a matching polo shirt under an open jacket, as well as a black baseball cap. The same outfit I'd seen on him at the mall weeks before, in fact—so it had been him. Next to him stood a girl more or less my height, and more or less my personal nightmare: cute, ponytailed, pretty, and exactly the kind of normal, non-freakish chick I'd fretted time and time again he might choose instead of me. Pondering the horror of it all, I didn't notice at first that they were dressed identically. "Then we can swing to Trenton Avenue and jet back here."

"Fine by me," said the girl.

"You have the coupons . . . Vick?" I'd been trying to sidle away, but I stopped in my tracks, paralyzed at the sound of my name. I'd been so sure they hadn't seen me! Only—wait. Their backs were still turned, I noticed in my frozen panic. Why in the world had he said my name, then? More important, why had he sounded so *guilty?* "Oh, jeez!" Gio started laughing aloud, confusing me further. He was staring at someone on the far side of the Dumpster. "Crazy! You look exactly like someone I know!"

Someone stepped out into view. For a second, I thought I was looking into a mirror—and then my brain caught up and I realized it was Tabitha. Even Gio was mistaking her for me! "She does look an awful lot like Vick," said the girl. "Eerie!"

Whether she meant the uncanny resemblance was eerie, or whether she thought I was freaky, I never found out. Tabitha looked away from the black-clad couple over to where I stood, noticing me for the first time. "Addy asked me to tell you she had to move the car," she said carefully, as if she wasn't certain what was going on. That made a nice even two of us. "A cop came and said we were in a no-standing zone."

I felt a shiver of fear when Gio's neck began to move. Slowly and surely, he turned his head to follow Tabitha's gaze, until at last our eyes met. I wanted to melt away into the ground like some Vick-shaped sculpture of brown sugar doused with hot water. I wanted to run as fast as my legs could carry me. I wanted to shatter into a million pieces and leave nothing behind save for my clothes. Tabitha would probably snatch them for her own, anyway. Instead, though, I hardened myself from the inside out, crossed my arms, and stared back. "Vick," Gio said to me, honestly gobsmacked.

"Thanks, Tabitha," I said, clearing my throat so that I sounded confident and cool. "But why don't you tell Addy I said it was okay to get back to Ray. I'm fine on my own."

For a second I thought she might toss off the heavy, dark persona she'd been playing to the hilt all afternoon; it really looked as if she might rush to my side and try to hug me, or something similarly dire. Instead, perhaps by frantic telepathy on my part, she finally nodded and stalked off.

During the exchange, Gio hadn't taken his eyes from me. I took two steps forward and nodded at the boxes he and the girl both carried. "Pizzas?" I asked. He nodded, a sick look on his face. I had the upper hand, here—the element of surprise, so vital in pulling off any sleight of hand. "You have a job delivering pizzas?" Again, he nodded.

"Um, why don't I go wait in the car?" said the girl, giving me a nervous look. Apparently she knew exactly who I was, though I didn't recognize her at all. Way to go yet again, Vick. She bobbed down slightly to take his boxes on top of her own, and staggered toward the Mustang.

With nothing between us now but unspoken words, I took another step toward Gio. "How," he stammered, "how did you—?"

I shook my head. "Don't. That's not the issue."

He had the decency to look ashamed. "I know."

"So all this time," I said in a low voice, the kind I'd used a hundred times before when we'd had one of our private conversations with our arms around each other, "you haven't been volunteering at all? You've been working?"

"Vick, the car was expensive. More than I told my folks it was. I needed to make some cash to pay . . ."

I ignored the pleading in his voice, and raised mine. "This was all about the *car?*" Oh, man. I should've known. Boys and their cars! Part of me was so hugely offended at taking second place to a gleaming hunk of metal and moving parts that I couldn't help but sound bitter. "You lied to me so you could keep your *car?*"

He was helpless, now. Vulnerable. I'd never seen Gio's natural sunniness so totally stripped away. Seeing him hurt made me ache. "Vick, please . . ."

"I don't understand. How can you be here and at the senior center at the same time?" I asked. "They think you're in the clinic even as we speak." He turned his head. "Did you sign in and then sneak out? No, you couldn't do that for five hours at a time," I said, working it out aloud. "Do you have a secret twin? Wait—did you get someone else to volunteer for you? You're out here earning money while someone does volunteer work in your name?" His jaw jutted out defensively at the words. "That's it, isn't it? You had someone else pretend to be you, so you could get your damned certificate. Anyone could say their name was Gio Carson and the Sycamore Point staff wouldn't know the difference, would they? Who was it?" I could eliminate half the usual suspects simply because I'd been stalking Gio with them all afternoon. "One of your jock buddies? Nah, they wouldn't charm the pants off old ladies in the elevators, would they. It had to be someone who'd do what you asked and stick with it simply because it was you who did the asking. One of your many fans?" I was getting warm, I could tell. He stared out of the sides of his eyes at the sky, a patented Vick Marotti classic. "Little Tony," I said, knowing I was right.

"It was his idea. And what's the difference between my job and your job? They're both . . ."

Worst thing to say to me, ever. "Don't," I told him, angry now. "His idea or not, you went along with it, didn't you? Don't tell me it never occurred to you it wasn't wrong. You took advantage—you took advantage of a little kid—because he idolized you. Because you could. Because you were popular. And he wanted to be popular, too."

"It wasn't like that, Vick," he pleaded. "Listen."

"I can't talk to you right now," I said. I wanted to cry, but I wouldn't allow myself to do it in front of him. "You kept this secret from me. You're not even *allowed* to have a job."

"When *can* you talk to me?" he asked, holding out his arms. I'd hit the bull's-eye too many times; he was fighting back, now. "I really want to know. You talk about secrets? You're the most secretive person I know. It's like . . ." He threw his hands in the air and let them slap his hips. "Talking to a brick wall, sometimes."

"If I don't tell you things," I countered, "it's because you don't need my crap. Nobody needs to hear my crap. What, are you getting your jollies trying to make me the bad guy, here? You're the one who didn't tell me anything about this. . . ."

"How's that any different from you not telling me things? And don't say you don't not tell me stuff, because you admitted just now that you do." The tangle of that sentence kept me off-balance enough for a few seconds that I couldn't answer. He pulled his flat hand between us. "See? Brick wall. When are you finally going to open up?"

"Fine," I growled. "So now you *want* to know about how the powers that be at school have called a social worker down on my head, so she'll see exactly what a mess my house is and, I don't know, try to send me to foster care. That is, if my dad doesn't skip town first, drag me with him, and I never get to see you again. Is that what you want?" Brick wall, huh? I'd show him bricks. I'd lob them at him one by one, and see if he flinched. "You want to know about how scared I am that you'll walk off with some other pretty girl who's more like you? I'll give you that one, too." My words came out with controlled, concentrated ferocity—not loud, but fierce.

"Social worker?" he asked softly, pained.

"I told you that you wouldn't want to hear," I said, still sarcastic.

"Have you talked to him about it?"

"No! We don't talk about that kind of thing! We haven't said a word about my job at the novelty

174

shop, and I've been doing that for three months. But at least he knows I'm doing it, unlike your folks. My job's aboveboard. And I didn't ask anyone to pretend to be me."

He winced. I'd hit home. "But . . . that girl looked like . . ."

He pointed to where Tabitha had stood a moment before. I didn't want to go there. "Her idea. I *had* to get my job, Gio. Because with his part-time gig, after the rent my dad's income doesn't completely cover stuff like, oh, I don't know, electricity and food. So you know, that's why there've been no movies and dinners out for me, the last few months. I'm a free-lunch girl now. Woo-hoo!"

"Oh my God!" Gio said. Maybe I'd lobbed too many bricks in his direction; he looked positively battered. "Why didn't you say anything about any of this?"

In a cold fury, I spat out the words, "Maybe if you were *around* to talk to."

"That's totally unfair! You should have told me! I gave you plenty of chances! I even *asked* if something was wrong!" I hung my head, knowing he was right, but still glared at him through my dark-rimmed eyes. "Don't you trust me enough to know these things? Or is it because you thought I'd run if I knew? Is that it? You've always had this idea that we weren't going to last." How dare he? How dare he be so infuriatingly, annoyingly *preachy* at a time when I was the one who deserved to be angry? "So why bother to talk, when you've already written me off in that head of yours!"

"Untrue!" I yelled at him, not caring how loudly my voice echoed against the red brick of the alleyway. "Absolutely untrue!"

"Is it?" he asked, red-faced. "Tell me. You've never, ever thought to yourself that this—us—was going to be over once I head off to college?"

"Obviously you have!"

"I haven't," he retorted almost instantly, angry. "But apparently I'm the only one. You've always given us an expiration date. Autumn, next year. It's a hell of a lot easier to kiss what we've got good-bye than it is to clean up your act and see if we can have a future together. Good-bye, Gio! Hello, somebody else! Tired of one toy. Time for the next. Right?"

Our argument ground to a halt, bogged down by that one question. There wasn't anyone else. There wasn't! What did he think he knew? I couldn't ask outright. What was saddest was that at that moment, I really didn't care. Maybe he was right. Maybe we had a date stamp, and it had long since expired. Instinctively my hand groped for my rose quartz pendant. Of course, it wasn't there. I'd probably never see it again.

"I have never, ever treated you like a toy. I've never treated you like a possession." The voice coming from my lips frightened me. I sounded like a horror movie chick possessed by the devil, right before everything's all green projectile vomit and priests flying out of second-story windows. "I leave that to you. You're a brat, Gio. A brat!" His face, stony and stubborn, was a reflection of my own. "Everything you want, you get. Video games. DVDs. Cars. Friends. Admirers. Fans. Good colleges. Me."

"I've wo—"

"Don't you dare tell me you've worked for it," I
snapped. "We both know that there's at least one little certificate you didn't do any work for." He hung
his head, at last ashamed. "How did you get Tony to
do it? What'd you promise him? Rides in the Mustang?"

"I told him he could hang with me, whenever." Ah.
Popularity, then—a currency I could gratefully never
handle again in my lifetime. "And I bought him, you
know, comic books. The ones his mom wouldn't let
him have. He'd hang at the comic store after school,
pick out what he wanted, and I'd pick him up, buy
the stuff, and drop him at Sycamore Point." In desperation, he appealed to me with open hands. "I
know it was stupid. But Vick, you know my folks. You
know the *insane* pressure they put on me."

I knew. But I cut him off all the same. "I'm going,"
I told him, swiveling around on my heel. I'd return the
way I came, behind the Dumpsters.

"Vick!" He must have known he'd gone too far. He
sounded pleading. Regretful, even. "Don't be like
this."

"This is how I am." I stopped and sighed, and gave
him one last look. "Deliver your pizzas, Gio."

I heard him call a final time before I dodged around
the massive metal container and sprinted back to the
drive. I stumbled over the corner of a cardboard bundle and banged my wrist on the bricks, but I didn't
care. The pain at least gave me an excuse for the tears
in my eyes.

Half of me hoped that Addy had been obstinate

enough to ignore my instructions and that I'd find her circling the parking lot, waiting for me. No such luck. That was fine, I guessed. At least Ray wouldn't be stuck at the senior center worrying about his mom's car . . . not that I'd ever get another chance to ride in it again. Even if I stocked its glove compartment with a month's supply of Paydays, I suspected he wouldn't come pick me up out here in the middle of consumer-land. Sniffling to myself, I stumbled along the store-fronts until I happened on a pay phone outside the pet supply store. I considered it lucky that I had enough change in my pocket to make a call.

I'd learned the number only a week ago, but I knew it as well as any of my friends', or my own. "Yeah?" I heard on the other end.

"I'm kind of in a tight spot," I said to the boy, managing to keep the tears from my voice. "Can you help?"

"Yeah," said Tyler. "I'll be right there. You can count on me."

CHAPTER TEN

"Just one trick," Martina pleaded. Or at least, she delivered the request in what was as close to pleading as she probably ever got—a scowly, hands-on-hips, pouty kind of pleasing. On a better day, I would almost have thought it was cute. "Pleeeeeeeeease!" Working with kids wasn't too bad a deal. When they were enthusiastic about something, they sure let you know it.

The little kids, anyway. Once they got bigger, they turned into me: big, tight-lipped shut-ups who'd rather cut off a limb than let someone know something mattered, even when keeping quiet ruined everything. "Sorry, Charlie," I told her, reaching through the backroom door and grabbing my coat off the hook inside. "I'm on my way home."

"Home? It's only twelve-thirty!" she complained.

"I've got stuff to do," I told her. Like, an entire house to clean from top to bottom, so that when the social worker appeared the next week, it wouldn't look like I lived in this town's one and only crack house. And doing it in a way that wouldn't arouse my dad's suspicions, too. "I'll be in tomorrow from . . ."

She didn't give me a chance. "*One* trick!"

I sighed. Mr. Schecter had already given me the go-ahead to leave; he really wouldn't expect me to stick around for one eleven-year-old customer whose record purchase so far had been a whopping $7.75 two months before. Still, though. She'd come to see me. Rotten as I felt, I owed Martina something for that. "One trick," I agreed. "What'll it be? You want to see the pencil-through-the-card illusion again?"

She grimaced. "That is so lame."

"Didn't figure it out yet, huh?"

"No." Her pigheadedness got a grin out of me. "But I will. Anyway, I don't want you to show me a trick. I want to show *you* one."

That was an entirely different matter. Half a minute later we were over by the magic novelties counter, my coat draped over its end. "As you can see," she said, brandishing an old scrap invoice I'd provided, "we have a perfectly ordinary piece of paper."

"Yes, indeed!" I turned the sheet over when she offered it for examination. Never mind that I'd handed it to her only seconds before. Practicing audience interaction was good experience.

"And with this pair of perfectly ordinary scissors, I'm cutting . . ." Martina's face was all concentration as she bent the paper in two and laboriously cut a half-moon at the fold with a pair of fur-handled pinking shears from a nearby rack. When she held up the paper again, it had a more or less perfect circle in its middle. She stopped biting her lip and resumed. "A perfectly ordinary hole."

I nodded. She was, as Tabitha Hunter might have said in a previous, less post-Goth existence, absolutely adorable. "Now what?"

"I am going to perform a feat so remarkable that you will not believe your eyes!" she announced, laying on the hammy performer's voice. "First, I will need an ordinary playing card!" In a stage whisper, she added, "I have one in my pocket if you need it."

"Okay," I whispered back, and let her slip it to me discreetly. "Why, Martina, I happen to have a perfectly ordinary playing card right here!" I said in equally fake a tone, pretending to produce it from my shirt.

"Thank you, audience member!" said Martina, taking it back. I could have eaten her with a spoon, by this point. "Here's what I have to ask you, audience member: without tearing the paper or bending the card, can you put the card through the hole?"

"Let's see." I took both objects and made a show of examining them. "The card's a lot wider than the hole." When I placed the card's bottom against the paper, it overlapped the opening by a good half-inch on either side. I poked a corner through. No good. Secretly, I was enjoying the trick for the expression on the little girl's face: she was utterly happy. Nervous, yes. A little frightened. But happy. I used to feel joy like that in the middle of a magic trick, back in the old days. Performing made all the bad stuff in my life vanish, for a little while. "I can't bend the card or tear the paper, huh?" She shook her head. "How about if I tear the card into itty bitty bits and drop it through?"

The way she narrowed her eyes? Distilled, it would've been sheer sulfuric acid. "No tearing *anything*."

"That's better," I told her, handing back the equipment. "Cover every eventuality, because people are always going to look for loopholes."

"Okay," she said, accepting the criticism. Then, in performance mode once again, she boomed, "Impossible, you say? Observe!"

Once again she folded the paper so that its circle was a half-moon across its top. She inserted the playing card from underneath. Using her fingers, she slid first the left half of the creased paper, and then the right, over the card's edges, in much the same way someone might slide off a blouse over her shoulders and down her arms. The rules of the trick had said no bending of the card—but not of the paper. "Incredible!" I enthused, letting out some hearty handclaps. "Bravo! Bravo!"

She gloried in the applause until it ended. "You've seen that before," she accused.

I had. It had been one of the simple tricks in the first magic book I ever had. Did I tell her that, though, and ruin the feeling of the moment? Or did I hold it in and fib to her? I made a quick decision. "Yeah, I have," I admitted. Before her face could fall, though, I added, "But that's the best I've ever seen it performed. Honestly. Knowing a trick lets me concentrate on how well a person's doing it. You had confidence and stage presence. Great job!"

Had I hurt her with the truth? She considered my praise for a moment, nodded with a faint smile, and tucked the compliments away somewhere secret. I knew that sometime later, at a private moment, she'd take out the compliment and enjoy it. "Come on," I told her, nodding at the door. "I've got a bus to catch. I'll walk you out." When she skipped alongside me in the direction of the wall exits, chattering and trying to wheedle more secrets from me, I knew I'd done the right thing.

For once, anyway.

The bus stop nearest my house wasn't at all fancy, like the ones at the mall or near my school that had nice little domed shelters with benches. My stop was nothing more than a battered sign bent at knee level where some car had collided with it a long time ago. Behind it stood a gas station that had closed before we'd moved into the neighborhood. The morning's rain made it all the more depressing. If there had been a spot to put a sign saying WELCOME TO THE WRONG SIDE OF THE TRACKS, this would have been it.

And right where that sign would have stood, legs planted firmly in the sidewalk's wet center, was Tyler Woodwell. When I stepped down onto the exit steps, waiting to stop, he seemed to be scanning the bus expectantly, looking for me; his hands were plunged deep into his jeans pockets, as though the thick woolen turtleneck he wore wasn't enough to keep him warm. Gone was his usual cap. A mess of floppy curls spilled over his forehead and ears. When with a whoosh of exhaust the bus roared off behind me, I regarded him with crossed arms, uncertain why he was there, or how I felt about that. "Hey," he said, once it was quiet enough to speak.

183

I heyed him back. What did I feel, exactly? Not awkward. I'd mentioned to Tyler that I was taking off that afternoon for housework. Not stalked—he never gave off that creepy, clingy vibe of desperation, and since he lived less than a half mile from me, it wasn't as if he'd come far. No, I felt more of that mild rush of gladness that comes from seeing a familiar face when you're down, mixed with that gloomy knowledge that your mood's only going to drag them to your low level. "What," I asked him, "all year long you've been doing the wool cap thing, but you give it up on the coldest, cloudiest day of the year?"

"I had to wash it sometime," he said, shrugging.

"TMI," I told him, jerking my head so that he'd follow me.

We walked for a little while in silence, but it wasn't that weird, heavy kind of silence that begged to be filled. Neither of us seemed to feel an urge to make meaningless small talk so there'd be noise. It was comfortable, really. The way I felt with my other friends. And considering my mood . . .

He must have been reading my mind. After we'd turned the corner and headed down my street, where soggy leaves clogged the diamonds of chain-link fences, he cleared his throat and asked, "So I kind of did something. But I have to know . . . are you still real upset? About, you know."

"You can say his name, dope."

"Fine. About Carson."

I liked Tyler. I wanted him to keep liking me. Could I count on that if I burdened him with all my idiot problems? Of course, Gio had pinpointed that very doubt as my biggest fault. Maybe, if Tyler were offering, I could practice on him. "I was thinking about something on the way home," I told him, the words coming slowly at first. "There was this girl—a little girl, a fifth-grader—and she showed me this trick today. Magic trick," I explained. Suddenly curious, I added, "What did you do?"

"Never mind. Keep going." He nodded. "And I guessed that it was a magic trick."

At least he wasn't running. Encouraged, I plowed ahead. "Okay, this trick was really one of the simplest illusions around. I mean, it's not so much of an illusion as a brain teaser, really. But when she showed it to me, she was like, so totally into it that though I knew how the trick worked, I was holding my breath and hoping she'd pull it off. Because, you know, that's one of the things about watching a magician doing her act. You want her to succeed, right? Even when there's a really bad magician and he's dropping his props and not getting the timing right, or if he watches his hands, you still want him to make the trick work."

"Yeah," said Tyler, still with me. "It's kind of painful to see someone stumbling along."

"Not only that, but you want to think that illusion is possible—that it's not trickery. Don't you? You want to believe for a few brief seconds that it's possible to . . . I don't know." I was coming to an embarrassing revelation here. At least, embarrassing for someone with the kind of image I apparently had. "You want to believe

185

it's possible to overcome the limits of the boring old everyday grind and create something . . . you know. Truly magical."

"Like love." I jerked my head up at that, for a second thinking he hadn't been following me. Those were the last words I'd expected from his mouth. "It's kind of like love," he repeated, not looking at me. We crossed another street to my block, jogging to avoid a turning car before he spoke again. "You want to believe it's possible. Not a trick, or not someone else's issues and your own issues canceling each other out for a little while. You want to believe it can happen." He let out a little sigh, soft as a kitten. "Even when you know it can't. Or won't."

"Yes. That's exactly the way it feels with . . ." It wasn't until I looked over at his stricken face that his words hit home. Like me, he seemed mortified at having said something wrong. We weren't talking about the same things. I was talking about Gio and me. He was talking about an entirely different couple. "Oh, Tyler." I sounded like the saddest person in the world.

He shook his head, then reached out to rip a remaining leaf off a bush overhanging the sidewalk. "Don't," he warned.

"You and I—"

"I said, don't." His hands reached automatically for his head, as if he had intended to pull his cap down around his ears. With nothing there, though, he had to curl his hands into fists and stuff them back into his pockets. "I shouldn't have opened my mouth."

"Oh, that's crap." I was determined to keep it light. "We're friends. Say anything." Despite my permission, he didn't. "Please don't turn this into a big thing. You know I like you."

"But not that way?"

I battled for words. I didn't need this discussion. I could've and should've left him there in front of the rusted-out lawn swing in front of the house next to mine and run home in a huff. Somehow, though, I thought Tyler deserved better. Besides, I couldn't answer his question with a flat-out no. I turned and faced him. "Gio and I have unfinished business," I said carefully. "I don't know what's happening there. I have to find out before I make any decisions."

"The dude lied to you, Vick," he said. I could hear pain in every syllable.

"I wasn't all that truthful with him, either."

"He faked volunteer work." I felt my heart thump a little harder at hearing him say it aloud. As if reading my reaction, he quickly added, "I'm not going to say anything to anyone about it. You asked me not to. It's something to think about, that's all."

"Please don't be all depths of despair-y," I begged. "That's not a rejection."

His voice was barely audible as we walked on. "It's not rejection that hurts most. I can survive despair. It's . . . it's the hope, Vick." He cleared his throat several times, trying to rid himself of the lump I could hear there. "It's the hope that rips me apart."

So dumbstruck was I at Tyler's honesty that for a moment all I could do was gape at him, awestruck, grappling with what to say. For months I'd been traveling a road with Gio—bumpy now, for sure—and without any warning, I could easily envision myself branching off in a different direction entirely, with Tyler. Would that road be any easier to travel? My stomach tied itself into knots at the prospect. Would it be a road I wanted to take?

"Vick?" I heard from behind me. I turned. Gio had padded to the end of my sidewalk, his right hand clutching a broom handle. Had merely thinking about him summoned him to my side? No, the others were there as well, crowded around my front stoop in the distance. Addy, Brie, Ray, Dorie, Des, Tony, the dark smudge known as Tabitha . . . all of them and a few of Des and Dorie's friends as well, sitting there like they'd been waiting for me.

I looked from Gio to Tyler and back again, and knew I was at a crossroads without a map. "Woodwell." Gio wore the expression of someone who'd put one too many Lemonheads in his mouth.

"Hey, Carson." Tyler nodded, keeping it curt and short.

I panicked. How much of any of that conversation had Gio heard? "What . . . what are you guys doing here?" I stammered.

Funny how though I'd never done a thing with Tyler, never voiced anything disloyal about Gio to him, I felt like a big, fat cheater. Maybe it had been that one, brief glimpse of a road that didn't have Gio as a passenger, or maybe it had something to do with my own fault in our last argument. Either way, it brought a shade of red to my face impossible to miss. "We all kind of came to help out," Gio told me. *Surprise* wasn't strong enough a word for my reaction. Add a few metal tubes around my hanging, swinging jaw, and you'd have an industrial-strength wind chime. "Tyler told me you were cleaning up today. So I got everybody to come."

"I thought you could use the extra help," Tyler quickly added. "I tried to tell you, but then we got, you know. Sidetracked."

I stared at him, alarmed, dismayed, and more than a little awed. He'd arranged all this for me? With his rival? "You shouldn't have done that," I said in what felt like slow-motion video. The words took eons to say. During that time, both Addy and Ray straggled across the still-wet lawn. I could see that Addy carried some kind of duster, while Ray's toolbelt had clipped to it every spray cleaner known to mankind. "This is my problem." No, that was wrong. Hadn't I learned my lesson about shutting people out of my life? Look in what trouble that had landed me! I tried again. "I don't want to put you guys . . ."

"Vick?" Ray settled one hand on a plastic tube of glass wipes and the other on a bottle of Scrubbing Bubbles. "Shut up."

"Seriously!" I said, voice raised at the sight of Addy's smug face. Ray shook his head. "My dad . . ."

"He's taking a nap, from what we could tell," Addy said.

"Tony looked through the windows," Ray explained.

Addy nodded. "We'll be quiet."

"You've got better stuff to do than spend all afternoon in our mess."

"Vick?" Addy used the same tone as Ray, earlier. She pointed to her cheek. "Tear."

If they all turned into Tabitha clones, I'd kill them. "Keys, please," said Ray, holding out a hand.

What could I do? I handed them over with a sinking conviction that by sundown, whether I liked it or not, my dad would wake up and find himself in a bubble-scrubbed bungalow complete with sparkling windows and, guessing by the packages Tabitha clutched as she propped up the front door, a new shower curtain and bathroom rug. The place might eventually be clean enough to convince a social worker I wasn't in immediate danger of cholera or leprosy. "You guys suck," I said, trying not to cry.

Addy gave me a quick hug and swatted me on the butt with her duster. "Yeah, we love you too." She leaned over so quickly that for a second I thought she might plant a quick kiss on my cheek. She was affectionate like that. Instead, her lips stopped an inch away from my right ear. "Want to repay me? Talk to Gio," she said, adding, "At least listen to him. Promise?"

I nodded, then shrugged. It probably looked like I was cringing. I was. Now that they had the keys, everyone seemed to be melting away in the direction of the house. Seriously, it was eerie, like someone had blown an invisible whistle to cue everyone to move. Tyler lingered a moment, then nodded at me and began loping away as well. What an enormous favor he'd done. Like it or not, I was immensely touched. It made me all the more nervous that Tyler was deserting me, leaving me alone with Gio for the first time in days.

Would he be apologetic? Was I going to have to

make the first move? Was one of us going to say something else we'd regret, later on? Not that I was sorry for the things I'd said the other evening. They'd all been heartfelt. I regretted that any of it had to happen, though. Here I'd been worrying that my distrust was the thin edge of the wedge driving us apart, yet apparently the things we'd chosen not to say to each other had begun it long before. I knew why Addy had made me promise to stay; walking away from Gio would be a lot easier than actually having to figure out what to talk about.

I cleared my throat. He shoved his hands in his pockets. So certain was I that I would have to be the first to speak that I began to say, "So. . . ." while trying to figure out how to follow it up.

Gio thrust out his right hand. Dangling from it was a gold chain and a pink stone that I immediately recognized: my rose quartz pendant. He tilted his head. "The stone was kind of wedged down in the leather sofa in the Jerome's pool room," he said, his voice raspy and strained. "I never found the chain. Somebody else might have picked it up or something. I don't know. So I got a new one. I hope it's okay." His words grew softer and softer. "Are you going to take it?" he finally asked, when I didn't move.

"Yeah," I said, holding out my hand. He let the stone fall into my upturned palm. The cold length of metal chain pooled around it. I was so glad to see that pendant again. I know in movies and things women are always throwing away jewelry that their ex-boyfriends gave them, but I didn't feel like doing that. My first instinct, honestly, was to put it right around my neck. But what would that have told Gio? And what did the impulse mean? "Thanks."

"I know what you're thinking," he said, hand going back into his pocket. "I can't buy my way out of this one. This doesn't make everything right. You were right, I'm a brat."

"Gio." I couldn't stand the thought he might have been flogging himself with that one word I'd so carelessly thrown out. "I didn't mean . . ."

"You did," he said quietly. "And you were right." A long silence followed, while he composed himself. At long last he looked up at me. "I'm trying to fix things."

"Well, okay," I said, putting the necklace in the front pocket of my jacket. "Thank you."

"Not the pendant," he corrected. "That's the least of it. The mess with the senior center is what I meant. It was insane to think I could get away with it. You were right about everything. I was cocky. I was a *total* brat. So I took Little Tony to the center and 'fessed up." I whistled through my teeth. "Yeah, kind of rough. Not as rough as telling my mom and dad, though."

"Oh man," I said, imagining the fireworks. Gio could do no wrong in the Carsons' eyes. "I bet."

"Yeah, especially since they didn't want me having a job to distract from school and stuff." He shrugged and looked away. "I quit the pizza place. Had to. Now I'm going to have to sell the car, since I kind of, you know, lied about it and everything."

Ouch. That would hit him right where it hurt. The

Mustang had been my rival, pure and simple, but I'd never wanted anything to happen to it. Outside of the crazy fantasies of falling pianos and unexpected rock-slides I'd had the night after our fight, anyway. "I'm really, really sorry," I said, meaning it.

"God, Vick. What got me so crazy? Everything used to be so simple."

"I know," I told him. I felt compelled to speak. "You're not the only crazy one. I mean, you didn't carjack anybody, at least." Apparently neither Ray nor Addy had filled him in on that particular exploit, because he shook his head, blank-faced. "Never mind."

"So you and Tyler . . . ?" A new note had crept into Gio's voice, harsh and cracked. "Not that it's any of my business."

"No. God, no, Gio." I don't know what irritated me more—that he asked, or that he assumed I wouldn't answer.

"If you and he . . . I mean, you'd tell me if there's anything. Right?"

He stared at me. I stared at him, and then at the appearance of Brie on my front stoop to shake out what looked like the rag rug that lay in front of the TV. She was craning her head, obviously hoping to overhear something. Finally I looked back at Gio again. "The silence you hear? It isn't me not telling you anything," I said at last, painfully afraid I sounded incoherent. "It's me telling you there's nothing." Maybe hope was the worst emotion in the world. Gio's expression seemed wracked by it. The dope never really could keep a good poker face. "Honestly."

He nodded. "Well. Even if. I couldn't really blame you. I mean, he's no *me*, but . . ." The faintest hint of a grin graced his handsome mouth. "Joke," he reassured.

I couldn't take it so lightly. "Not laughing. Sorry about that."

He seemed to understand. Brie, who from a distance had been watching the two of us with speculation without witnessing a smoochy reconciliation or a slap across the face, finished shaking the rug and moved reluctantly back inside, probably to tell the others what little she'd seen. "So are we together still? Is it another wake-up, not a break-up?"

Having my own words lobbed in my direction made me wince. "I don't know yet," I said, trying not to sound defeating. The end result sounded, well, sad.

That wasn't good enough for Gio. "Are we apart? I won't want—crap." I shook my head again. I didn't want that, either. "Do you need to be with someone else? With Tyler?"

"Gio!" He exasperated me. I had too many questions of my own. How was I supposed to answer his, too? "I don't *know* what I want. How can I know what I want when I don't know where I'll be in a month? A week? What if Dad decides tomorrow to pick up and head to, I don't know, Nevada? Nothing I say today will be any good. Don't you understand?" I'd never sounded so hopeless in my life.

"He's been depressed since your mom died," said Gio. Well, duh! I waited for him to tell me something I didn't know. "Maybe starting over somewhere new invigorates him for a while, gets him out of his blues. What've you done the other times he wanted to move?"

I threw my hands in the air. "Moved! I didn't have a choice!"

"Did you tell him you didn't want to?"

His suggestion left me dumbstruck. Of course I hadn't. In every other city, at school I'd been Vickie The Meek And Picked-On. I couldn't wait to start again. Now, though, I couldn't bear the thought of leaving. "No, I didn't."

"You should say something this time, Vick." While Gio spoke, my hand slipped into my pocket and clutched at the pendant there. Some curious feeling gnawed at my insides. "How's he going to know what's important if you don't tell him?" The pain blossomed, setting my stomach churning. My heart beat out of rhythm. "I mean, God. Not because of us. Not for my sake, no way. Because of school. Because of your friends. Because . . . you've hit a stride here. Haven't you? You should tell him it's important to you. For once."

I looked at him slowly, my hands cradling my hurt stomach. I knew the painful emotion for what it was: hope. "Do you think he'd listen?"

"Only one way to find out. Right?"

Gio was so sweet and confident that I wanted to hug him right there. I couldn't, though. I wasn't the kind of girl who indulged in sudden gestures of—oh, the hell with it. I think Gio was astonished when out of nowhere I grabbed him around the shoulders and squeezed the stuffing out of him, but I didn't care. I'd seen in Tabitha the dark side of Vick, and that glimpse was more than enough to turn me into an occasional hugger. "What was that for?" he asked, huffing for breath.

"For being you," I told him. "And for believing in a world where you get everything you ask for."

"Oh."

Once again, I saw the hope in his expression. Gio liked a tidy ending. A happy ending, too. I didn't have one to give him—not yet. Already I'd made tracks across the wet grass toward the house. "Later," I called out. "I promise we'll talk. I have to do this now," I told him. "Before I lose my nerve. Or before it's too late."

He nodded. Good old Gio. Maybe he really did want to fix things. And Tyler? Well, he'd been the one to pull together all this kindness. They both wanted the best for me, in their own ways. Maybe, just maybe, I could wrangle a solution from my current mess in which I had some difficult choices to make about my future. That would be a heck of a lot better than no choices at all.

Inside the house, I could hear Brie and Addy and Ray arguing in low voices about what to do with the stack of take-out menus sitting on top of the microwave. Later, I'd tell them to ditch them. For now, though, I had to talk to my dad. I had to let him know that though bad stuff had happened, I didn't intend to start over again. At least, not somewhere else. I wanted the both of us to start all over again right here in this one-horse, two-bit, three-stoplight, Godforsaken town, where for the first time I had people I wanted to keep in my life.

Outside Dad's bedroom door, one of Dorie's friends was busy plucking the dead leaves from a spider plant that, by the law of averages, should have given up the ghost long ago. She looked up and jumped at the sight of me, looking so much like a startled rabbit that I had to stop. "Hey," I said gently. I took in her long brown hair, her worn sweater, the clogs that clattered on the floor with every shuffle, but couldn't bring to mind a name. "You're . . ." I prompted.

"Sorry!" She cringed as if expecting me to finish that sentence with, *You're a peon!* or *You're in my freakin' way, moron-girl!*

"No, I mean, what's your name again?"

The sad truth was that I'd never bothered to learn it. With any luck, she might think it had momentarily slipped my mind. Was the polite social lie working? It was. "Anne," she said, still shy.

She looked like an Anne. "That's right. Anne," I said, committing it to memory and giving her a smile. From then on, I vowed to myself, I wasn't going to be a person who coasted through life, counting on everyone to know my name when I didn't bother to learn anyone else's. I was going to bother. I was going to give a damn. That submerged part of the social iceberg? Better watch out. Vick Marotti intended to get to know each and every one of you.

Even if it meant risking, you know, a little popularity. Of the right kind, this time.

The little rabbit still watched me. "Well, Anne," I said, my hand on the knob of my dad's door. "As of

197

today, I officially owe you. Count on it, okay?" She nodded rapidly and like the frightened bunny she was, scampered off to leave me alone.

Then again, maybe I wasn't so alone. Every room of the house held someone who cared about me. Both Tyler and Gio had jogged my memory with that fact. It was high time I reminded my father of it, too. I took a deep breath and knocked on his door. "Dad?" I said tentatively, popping it open. The afternoon's first sunshine slanted sideways through his blinds, cutting through the gloom within. "Dad?" I repeated, sliding inside. "I have to tell you something."

It was time we faced a few truths. It was time to talk.

NAOMI NASH
SENSES WORKING OVERTIME

Kaylee's on the edge of catastrophe. To help a friend, she cuts summer school and ventures solo into New York City, just in time for the decade's worst blackout. To make matters worse she has *synesthesia*—the connections in her brain are messed up, so she can't trust her senses. She can't be more in the dark.

Closing her eyes, Kaylee makes a leap of faith. She decides to follow Ramon, the dangerous-looking boy whose voice smells like honeysuckle. But that's just the start. To beat her father home, she has seven hours to overcome crowds, chaos, carjackers, a relentless stalker…and an intense attraction to a boy who should be wrong but feels so right.

Dorchester Publishing Co., Inc.
P.O. Box 6640
Wayne, PA 19087-8640

_____5404-3

$5.99 US/$7.99 CAN

Please add $2.50 for shipping and handling for the first book and $.75 for each additional book. NY and PA residents, add appropriate sales tax. No cash, stamps, or CODs. Canadian orders require $2.00 for shipping and handling and must be paid in U.S. dollars. Prices and availability subject to change. **Payment must accompany all orders.**

Name: _____

Address: _____

City: _____ State: _____ Zip: _____

E-mail: _____

I have enclosed $_____ in payment for the checked book(s).

CHECK OUT OUR WEBSITE! www.dorchesterpub.com
_____ *Please send me a free catalog.*

Didn't want this book to end?

There's more waiting at **www.smoochya.com**:

Win FREE books and makeup!
Read excerpts from other books!
Chat with the authors!
Horoscopes!
Quizzes!

 smooch   Bringing you the books on everyone's lips!